WHY DO MEN CHEAT

What Women Need To Know Before Dating A Guy

PURE SERIES BOOK ONE

A NOVEL BY

R. L. WINECOFF

DILLARD & WINECOFF PUBLISHING

Copyright © 2019 by Dillard & Winecoff Publishing, LLC

Designed by: R L Winecoff via Canva

Manufactured in the United States of America

10 9 8 7 6 5 4 3 2 1

ISBN 978-1-38-818364-6 (Paper Back)

ISBN 978-1-38-818364-6 (Ebook)

www.rlwinecoffjr.com

DEDICATION

I dedicate this to Arriciana, Zhynasia, Korea, Tamyra, Mason, and Angel. May1 your imagination lead you to your true selves.

FORWARD

———————

B efore I get into this, I want to make clear of a few things, and apologize for a couple. Hmmm...that sounds bad already. This was not inspired by some hate-filled failed relationship I had or am experiencing to create this "how to/what to". As a matter of fact, my experience in the dating world is just about as average as average can be, positioned to normality. I have loved, I have hurt, I have lost, I have had fun, and I've played as if I wasn't hurt in front of my friends so I wouldn't be ridiculed or called a punk. Really?! What guy in the world wants to sit around that kind of firing squad after he bragged about how amazing he was, then get dropped like a bad habit? Nope!

I'm just a regular guy, who has regular friends, a lot being women, that I talk to from time to time for advice just like any other God-fearing American. I'm not good in math, I can't remember how old my parents are, I can't name all of the presidents of the United States, I like all genres of music, I am a Carolina Panthers fan, I still think the term "fartknocker" is the funniest term ever created, I've thought I was God's gift to women, and no matter how hard I try, I still fail at being an expert on

i

women. Oh! I'm also an entrepreneur that created an app, run a festival, and deal with buying diamonds.

Now, with that being said, I also dabble in putting my elaborate opinion on paper, hoping its "catchy" enough for people to treat it as if it was the right opinion to agree with, which would give me more confidence, promoting my literacy. I am not a doctor, specialist, expert, consultant, nor counselor on this subject. I have not conducted a field survey, followed guys storming out of apartments, or held listening antennae in an unmarked van, outside a public park, where a nice lady was left sobbing on a bench. I'm not a psychologist, sociologist, or master dater.

This is starting to sound very much like a disclaimer. Anything you read is only my opinion of how I see the topic. Please do not go waving this book in some poor shmucks face screaming, "Is this what you did to me?" Do not go all bat shit crazy and jack up the alimony, nor child support payments because what you read may seem identical to your own experience, past or present. Do not go "two can play that game", and assume your current companion is ducking off on you, then attempt to beat him to the punch. Guys I would like to apologize if this happens to you but understand you will bounce back.

Do not get dressed in all black camo, no matter how hot you look, and spy while you're always promoting singleness, "I'm a good woman", "I don't need a man"..."Oh! He bought you flowers?!", "I'm independent"..."What?! He forgot your birthday?!", girlfriend that tends to be overly dramatic and emotional. I'd like to apologize if you have such a friend. This is just some really great reading material to allow you to view dating from a different perspective. You could, or could not agree with it, which is completely fine, because, at the end of the day, no one gets this stuff right anyway. It's always a roll of the dice...life...no matter whom or what it's pertaining.

Do we want the fairytale of happily ever after? But of course, yet some journeys don't make it. And that's just reality. Get used to that word, REALITY, by the way. It will allow you to grasp and identify the uncommon reasons why men cheat. This isn't to hurt men; this is to help you not hurt yourself with men that are not trying to hurt you. Bet you didn't see that one coming. Truth be told, men seem to cheat for a number of reasons. They cheat because they are not secure, conversation isn't appealing, become attracted to someone else, the sex isn't good anymore, he is depressed, he has mommy issues, he's scared, non-committable, he doesn't know

(...literally), not ready to settle down, he's married, your kids are bad to him, finances, etc.

The list goes on and on, and I would know because I am an ex-cheater. I am not afraid to admit it although I am not proud of it. It's nothing to be proud of because most women want to know why you are no longer in a relationship and will less likely choose to date you knowing that you cheated because they are afraid it can happen to them also. Although you don't want to hear a man has cheated, you actually need to, but we will touch that later on in the book. This will be raw and to the point, so don't think I'm going to drag it out with some exasperated, elaborate theory. It's all real reasons, with real situations, about why men cheat...period.

REASON ONE

HE'S YOUR TYPE

L et just start with the number one reason a guy cheats on you. Dunn dada dunnn! He's your type. Yes! Yes! I told you, you wouldn't see this coming. Women have a tendency to set themselves up for failure with this age-old love starter, and this tends to hurt more women when compared to the number of times it has succeeded. You've found yourself wanting Mr. Tall Dark & Handsome. Big hands, big feet, nice smile, and chiseled body grrr. Yet, the truth is he, Mr. Tall Dark & Handsome will cheat on you 65% of the time. This does not apply to all men, so please don't go giving guys strife. Yet, Mr. TDH has a high success rate of attracting women than Mr. SLD…Short Light and Decent.

How many times have you told yourself, "I want a tall guy so I can wear heels?", code for a guy who "looks" like he can protect me. In comparison. Finding a true TDH is almost as good as your chances of winning the lottery. Mr. TDH has a plethora of women seeking him out which demotes your ability to keep his attention. Look at the approach of "law of averages". For every 10 people a salesman sees, he's likely to close one. So, if Mr. TDH is a good salesman, i.e. nice car, job, education, chivalric, and smells good, then Mr. TDH has a woman he can replace you with every 30 minutes for the next 48 hrs. Why does he cheat? He's your type and not your substance.

TDH can't help his genetics, but what he can help is who he allows entering his life. With all of those options a guy, no matter who, no longer sees himself as a sex symbol, but as someone who has more to offer. He also has experience in weeding out bs women so when you're thinking "my type" he's probably labeling you a "one night". TDH doesn't need arm candy, he needs arms to handle. Get rid of the "**type**" mentality because the reality of a "**type**" does not define substance, it defines physical. Types are just vague descriptions of what you want, not necessarily what you need.

Although a TDH may not know this directly, there is a great chance that he has enough experience to know what you're going to be even before he says hello. Be mindful because tall dark and handsome is really a true damn heartbreaker.

LOVE DO US PART

"**W**hy do you have to be so negative Kim? I thought you would be more supportive. This is important"

"I am supportive of you Jenna and have been as your best friend since 7th grade when you kissed Tariq under the bleachers. I told you he was too advanced for you because he had a reputation for getting girls to touch his ding-a-ling. But did you listen to me then? No! You kissed him anyway and his ding-a-ling got hard...no wait...his finger."

"Girl shut up about that my goodness it's been ages. You just will not let it go."

"Hell, I'm not the one that didn't let it go based on what he told the whole 7th grade I mean were you really that naive Jenna?"

Jenna could almost feel herself relive that moment at school in the gym. She kissed the cutest boy in her school for the first time and his penis got hard. She touched it, and for some reason wouldn't let it go. Thinking back, she had her eyes closed, it was cold that day. She thought it was just his finger in his gloves. When she stopped kissing him, which seemed like forever, she looked down, shy from the kiss, to see her hand on his penis.

"Please, Kim."

"No please Jenna! You got picked on by everyone after that, and I thought you would never come back to school. I stood by you and I told him he was a jerk for doing that to you. Now I'm saying it again. You've worked so hard to make partner at that firm. You deserve it. But it's a male-dominated firm and those guys have been stringing you along. I just don't want you to get your hopes up."

Jenna put her right palm on her forehead while she held her office phone with her left hand. Deep down she knew Kim was right. She worked hard to get to her position at the law offices of Royal Oak at Garden. She was top of her class at Columbia and spent countless hours at the office which resulted in the firm winning some of his biggest cases and landing some of its biggest clients. They just had to promote her.

She had no kids and she had no time for a relationship. She would have to be successful first then find her dream guy. A guy that can fit her life like a glove. Someone who achieved equal, or more in their lives as she had. She wanted what most women want in a guy. Successful, tall, dark, and handsome. Yet all of that would have to wait especially if today didn't go as she hoped.

Although she was being considered, talk around the office was that the partners were going to promote Charles Russell, a kiss-ass who was always going out of his way to be snooty with her... prick. Then there's Melvin Bostic who actually went to law school with her and came from a prominent family. He could have joined his dad's firm, but Melvin wanted to make his own way which she admired. Last was Kristen Garden, daughter of Marco Garden, senior partner. Kristen was the real deal, despite her father's seniority. She held her own, and Jenna felt an honest challenge with her.

She knew both were fighting the same girl fight and for that reason alone she had an untold sisterhood with her, and always would. Not today though, today she wanted that promotion and she did not want that bitch to have what she so longed for. Hell, Kristen already had Brandon Matthews, a 6'2 chiseled Apollo in the flesh. Brandon came from a prominent family too and attended Harvard Law. He was on the rowing team, and at 45 looked as if he was at his peak fitness. The first time Jenna met him, he towered her 5'6 frame with his long-tailored Armani suit. He smelled of Chanel de Bleu, and his hands were strong yet soft.

She sometimes fantasied about how easy he could pick her up and enter her in the middle of the room. The thought made her moist, and her nipples erect.

"Jenna!" Kim said on the phone

"Yeah?"

"Did you hear what I said?"

"Yeah Kim, I heard you."

"If you get it cool, but if not don't beat yourself up about it okay?"

"Okay I won't"

She knew that she would.

"Promise me, Jenna."

"I... I promise Kim I won't."

"Now are we still meeting at the gym today?" Kim asked.

Just when Jenna was about to reply, Kelly her secretary, walked in and said, "Excuse me, Ms. Frazier, the senior partners would like to have a word with you." Jenna nodded in affirmative then cut off Kim.

"Kim they just summoned me, I have to go, but I will call you back okay?"

"Okay, Jenna good luck and remember what I said okay?" 'Okay!" Jenna responded then hung up.

She took in the moment with a deep breath, told herself she got this, stood, and began her way up to the 26th floor. She was only on the 23rd. Her firm occupied 10 floors of a building in the heart of Manhattan. It was just one of six locations the firm had. They were titans of law firms, and it showed. She was looking to join in on such a legacy. When she reached the 26th floor it was nothing like she had seen before, as she had never been up there. No one except the partners and their priority clients. Sheila Vaughn stood by the double frosted doors pointing.

"Right this way Ms. Frazier they are expecting you." The marble was white as snow and shined like glass. The whole floor was panoramic views of the New York City skyscraper skyline. There was a large red oak conference table that looked to have 20 chairs on both sides, with three larger chairs at the head. It was the most intimidating scene that she had ever seen. No, it was the second. The first was the three senior partners sitting in the chairs staring right through her soul. She could feel her armpits start to perspire. Her heart beat faster and faster as she began to flush red in the face.

"Would you like something to drink Miss Frazier?" Sheila asked. "No thank you, I'm fine thanks." Sheila nodded and walked backward closing the doors behind her.

Jenna turned back looking at the three men who were going to break her heart or change her life staring at her. They sat eyeing her for a minute before Ed Royal's deep voice boomed through the room for her to have a seat. They all had folders in front of them no doubt having reviewed her fate. Then Bill Oaks said, "Let's get started, shall we?" Jenna felt faint.

PURE LOUNGE 11 pm

Tinging of a fingernail hitting a champagne flute

"Excuse me! Excuse me! May I have everyone's attention? I would like to make a toast. " Kim said. "I'd like to toast to my best friend since 7th grade, sister, and new partner of Royal Oaks and Garden."

Jenna stood with her just the two of them and toasted to her making partner. All that work paid off, she made partner she thought to herself, and she deserved it. She called her parents back in North Carolina, who were excited to hear the news. They promised to come for a visit in the following weeks.

"So, what are you going to buy with that new 7-figure salary of yours? Or is it 8 figures? Shit, how rich did you become today?" Kim said while sitting and leaning as the second bottle of Belaire Rose started kicking in.

Even though it was only the two of them at Pure Lounge on the second level in VIP, and at a table for two. Pure was a nice upbeat lounge that was often frequented by a diverse crowd ranging from athletes, executives, entrepreneurs, actresses, actors, and underworld successes. It was the place you always saw in magazines or in the news that someone famous was coming to or from. Robert Louis, the billionaire owner of the infamous Tuvuler app, made Pure the hottest lounge on the East Coast. Tuvuler made him the man around town in Silicon Valley. As usual, it was packed with the who's who, and Mr. Louis was one of Jenna's elite clients. She would never have issues getting in, unlike the hundreds that stood in line outside.

"I just have a really secure financial future, Kim," Jenna said.

She toasted again with Kim, took another sip, and they both laughed.

"Come on girl, let's dance," she told Kim, as the DJ played Jay-Z's hit "Change Clothes" featuring Pharrell.

Kim and Jenna started to let loose, both in designer cocktail dresses, Kim's from Louis Vuitton, and Jenna's from Noble Society. They both were on top of the world. Although celebrating Jenna's promotion to partner, Kim in her own right, was an upcoming actress who recently launched her acting career and just happened to be considered for a major part in a movie. Coming from a small town called Kannapolis North Carolina, they would be considered the 4th and 5th notably successful outside of Robert Louis, Dale Earnhardt Sr., and George Clinton. Kannapolis North Carolina used to be a thriving industrial city with much promise, but when the textile giants Cannon Mills and Pillowtex shut down so did the morale, and people left to find better jobs.

The city was hurt more when neighboring tobacco giant Philip Morris closed relocating to Virginia. It was almost like a ghost town that started to become crime-ridden, so the best bet was to leave and not come back unless you had to visit or attend a funeral...basically long enough to say hey and bye... 3 days... make it 2.

As soon as the beat dropped the whole lounge was on its feet. The song playing was topping the billboard and seemed to come out of nowhere. "Like This" by Moss was a feel-good anthem. It made a lot of people from different parts of the world change their perspectives from negativity to being positive. It was inspiring and even found its way into corporate commercials.

As they both were swinging their hair from side to side they noticed their bottle girl approach with another bottle of Belaire Rose. She exchanged the empty bottle for the full one, took the old glasses, and started to place new glasses as they both turned to see her changing napkins.

"Right on time," Kim said smiling. "I love this place. It's like they know exactly when to show, and when to leave you alone."

The young bottle server who was about 22, curvy in all the right places smiled, winked at them, and exited with the empty bottle, old napkins, and flutes, but not before filling their glasses. They toasted again and starred out to the bottom floor for a bit.

"So now that you have your dream career, you need to seriously get laid," Kim said, visibly tipsier.

"Don't horny coochie advise me Kim, I'm well aware of my lack of a good man in my life."

"You say don't horny coochie advise you, but that response, prude as it was, was a sure sign that you need the horny coochie advice that you seriously need to get dicked."

"Kim!" Jenna shouted. "Shut up." As people in the next section looked in their direction. Kim looked at them, smiled and turned her attention to Jenna.

"Girl you are so tired. When was the last time you had some?" Kim sat staring into Jenna's eyes with a go-ahead and lie expression.

"I get my needs met thank you very much, Kim. Life isn't about money and sex you know."

Kim looked at Jenna as if she had shit on her face. "Bitch please, who you think you talkin' to?"

Jenna looked shocked and said "Bitch?!" Questionably.

"Yes, bitch, who you think you talkin to? Jenna, you are the most overworked, successful person I know. I look up to you and admire you as well cause you are an inspiration, but I bet your new salary any man in here can see you haven't busted a proper nut in a long time."

"Is it that obvious?" She said looking shy.

"Hell, yes it's obvious girl, and it's shocking because I see all the guys that hit on you but you just pass them up."

"They are not my type."

"So! A guy doesn't need to be your type to make you have an orgasm, Jenna."

"All guys aren't meant for me." She said looking away.

"All guys don't have to be meant for you to make you cum either Kim retorted."

"It's not what I mean... I mean... I'm looking for a specific guy. A guy that meets my requirements in life in every aspect. Career, relationship, and socially. I want the total package, and I will not settle. Women across this country tend to settle for guys and when they realize it they are being called a mom and a dad. Then the woman has to play both roles because the guy ends up being a waste of time. I have a type, and I'm sticking to it."

When Jenna look back at Kim, Kim was looking at her cross-eyed over her glass. "I have a type, Jenna."

"Oh, Lord."

"I do Jenna; you want to know what my type is? Huh? You want to know?"

"I think I do Kim."

"Yeah! Because it's a dick, Jenna."

Jenna busted out laughing as well as Kim. "Nice warm pulsating thick veiny dick."

Two guys from the table beside them must have overheard them because they were laughing and holding a toast to them while smiling. Kim raised her glass in response then blew them a kiss. They blew kisses back to her.

"My God you're crazy girl."

"But you love my crazy ass though."

Jenna smiled...

"Bitch! Kim spat wide-eyed."

Jenna's smile immediately left her face. "Enough with the bitches okay? I get it."

14

Kim nodded behind her friend. When Jenna looked at Kim, then in the direction she was looking she saw exactly why she made the comment. In a low tone slumping her shoulders, she also said... "Bitch!" then took a big gulp of champagne. Jenna could not believe what she saw, just as much as she couldn't believe who she was seeing. She immediately turned away.

"Oh my God Jenna that's" Jenna nodded.

"And is that?" Jenna nodded.

"And did they just?" Jenna nodded again.

Jenna grabbed her purse and started to walk off from the table. Kim followed right behind her, but not before a cell phone took about 6 photos. As they were heading down the stairs they were met by one of the security guards. A 6'9 bear of a white guy named Bishop who was 1 of the 6 people on Mr. Louis's personal security detail. His weight will be about 340 lb. Also, he was an ex-football player.

"Ms. Frazier, Mr. Louis would like to have a word with you" he said.

"We were just leaving" Kim responded.

But as they stepped down a couple of steps he motioned his massive arms for them to follow. Two more guards of equal size showed up behind them. It was if the big big-bodied men surrounded them. She looked at Bishop and said "OK." and they followed the massive guy to the office of Robert Louis. Jenna looked back at the shocking sight that Kim brought to her attention still in disbelief but grateful she could not be seen through the human shields she was surrounded by.

They were escorted to the far right of the lounge, and up the red-carpeted stairs. There was a guard named Mondo at the top standing in front of a divider. The guard mouthed something in his wrist, put a finger to his ear, and nodded for the women to come through. He opened the panel on the wall, inserted a card, and a section of the wall slid open to the left revealing a large open office space.

You could see everyone in the club from the mirrored glass, but they couldn't see you. The chairs were large dark mahogany. The center table had a sculpture of a headless female body with her arms across her breast, holding her shoulders, with her legs crossed knees up to her elbows. A desk as large as a picnic table, the same color as the chairs, sat directly across from the window looking into the club.

To the left was a small fully stocked bar with a slender bartender. He was making small talk with a gorgeous woman who looked like a model. She had on a fitting red dress, with red-bottom black 6-inch heels. Her hair was long, bone thinned and jet black that fell down to what seemed to be the lower back of her 5'10, size 6 frame. She spoke with a South American accent. She looked in their direction as if to gauge them but turned back just the same making more small talk with the bartender.

"I hope you didn't mind my asking for you, but I couldn't get away from some last-minute work."

Robert Louis approached them in an all-black William Wilson tailored suit, double-breasted, with no tie. Robert was about 5'9, 220 lbs., and stocky. He looked much younger than 42 years of age. Money must have done him well for preserving his youthful looks as he could possibly pass for 24 years old. He had a humble tone that was very approachable, and warm. His Southern drawl slightly tracked his professional dialect. Robert was an attractive man who easily seemed to be with beautiful women even before his fortune. They all knew each other because they all grew up in Kannapolis North Carolina.

"Fatboy who you think you summoning? Don't be acting all snooty now that you done got you some money boy" Kim said.

They all laughed. She gave him a big hug as well did Jenna.

"I'm not messing with you Kim," he said, laughing.

"Ummm hmmm you know better too because I will have all of this you hear me?" she said, pointing her finger around the room.

The lady in the dress was staring at her. Kim saw her, stared back, and rolled her eyes.

"Where are my manners? Please allow me to introduce you to my friend Ms. Korina Rodriguez" holding his hand out for the Latin model. Korina stood, smiled, and said "Pleased to meet you", as she shook Jenna's hand. She reached for Kim's hand but Kim waved and smiled.

"Hello!" Kim said, before walking over to the bar.

"What would you like to drink?" Robert asked.

"I'm good." Jenna said, waving her hand. "I've had enough for tonight!"

Kim cut right in, "Where is that Joseph Shore? I know you have it, don't even act like you don't fat Fatboy." Kim said, leaning over the bar.

Drew the bartender looked at Mr. Louis and Mr. Louis nodded. He quickly reached down, opened the cabinet, and pulled out the $10,000 bottle of cognac.

"Pour us all one as we are celebrating, aren't we?" Mr. Louis said.

Jenna looked with surprise. 'How did he know' she thought to herself.

He then blurted out, "Your mom posted it on Tuvuler. I think she had it out before the press release."

"Wow, mama Vickey on Tuvuler?!" Kim said.

"I would hope so" he responded.

"Shut up Fatboy everybody is on Tuvuler boy. You did your thang with that" she smiled and gave him a high five.

It was a genuine compliment. It was true they all had grown up together and hung out before he went off to Texas. He came back to Huntersville, a city just minutes outside of Concord North Carolina. He wasn't successful then but was on the verge. He ended up working with some people and was set up to take the fall for an SEC violation. His wife left him for another guy and he ended up serving 5 years in a federal prison in North Carolina.

Instead of letting life get him down he focused and designed the app in his spare time. He was released, then pitched it to someone he knew that got behind him and the app took off. It became the biggest app next to Facebook, Instagram, Uber, and OpenDoor.

19

Word has it is that he sold it for 5 billion yet still stayed on board to help run the company plus be the face. The world was inspired by his story. He became bigger when he allowed people to get paid while being on his app. From that point on it was hard not know who Robert Louis was.

"Look who's talkin' Kim. I heard about you being considered for that lead role in The Queen with Don Castro. Girl you're going to have the world bowing at your feet."

"I know, and they should too because I cannot be around you two looking like a third wheel for the successful. I get that part, and I'm going to make sure the world remembers my name," she said toasting her glass.

"They will" Jenna joined in.

Drew set four shots in front of them and they all held one in their hands. They raised them, and Robert did the honors.

"Here's to our beloved sister, friend, and one of the most positive women on the planet. I spent many nights by myself feeling like I had no one when my wife left me. Yet you Jenna would always show me what real family was and did. I will never forget that. If I could ever do anything and I do mean anything just name it. To our sister and friend. Cheers."

They all touch glasses and took a drink. They all caught up for a bit and decided to call it a night. The four of them talked until the lounge closed and even helped with closing up. Kim chatted with Korina as Korina didn't sit well with her. Something was off about her and she wasn't going to allow her to break her friend's heart. As they were about to leave, Robert Louis turned to Jenna.

"By the way, I'm thinking of coming out with a new spirit line. I'm naming it after my grandfathers. Can you help me out with that?"

"Sure, I'll have Kelly set up the appointment when I get all the legal in order okay?"

The sleek black Bentley Mulsanne rolled up first in front of Robert Louis then Jenna's black BMW 750 came right behind.

She looked at him and said, "Not bad."

He responded, "Not bad yourself."

Kim came between both and said, "Which one of these is taking me home.?"

Before Jenna could speak Robert said, "The first one is taking us all. I'm not allowing you to drive home after drinking. I'll have Bishop follow in your car okay?"

She nodded and handed the big guy her keys. Kim called shotgun and cut Korina off before she could sit in the front. Robert opened the door for her. Kim smiled as she got in the car and could feel Korina's stare burning into her fuming...and she was.

"Anybody hungry?" He asked.

"I'm not." Jenna said.

"Me either" Korina responded.

Kim said she could but didn't want to be bloated when she woke up the next morning so she passed. Robert went ahead and dropped Kim off first, then Jenna. He pulled up in front of her Brownstone in East Village New York where virtually all the A-list resided. He walked her to her door and told her he will be in touch. He watched her until she walked in and then got into his car, and drove off.

Her brownstone was of a modern and classic décor...was not too chic or masculine. You would want to kick your feet up but mind your manners as well. She went into her office just to the right of the entry, logged onto her email account and scanned it. She decided she would finish upstairs while she changed out of her clothes and prepare her bath. Her heels were off in a flash, and up to her bedroom, she went.

"How are you babe?" she said to her bed which she was dying to get into. She pulled her email up on her laptop then started to undress. The form-fitting dress slid down her curves with ease as she stood beside her bed. She looked down at her mail and scanned it quickly to prioritize her responses.

Based on the subject lines she viewed most of the emails were congratulatory from associates, reporters wanting interviews, new cases ("already..." she thought), and clients wanting follow-ups. She thought as she slid off her thong that she would have Kelly get back to the reporters to set up the interviews and send a general thank you to the congratulatory compliments. As for the direct messages requiring follow-ups and new clients, she would do those herself. The good balance she thought. She opened her Tuvuler account and had 1663 notifications.

'I'm not even prepared for this yet" she thought to herself.

She walked into her huge custom bathroom and opted to take a hot water bubble bath, then take a shower. As she leaned to turn on the hot water her size D breasts hung paralleled. Her nipples were slightly erect she reached for her container of lavender bath beads and poured them in the filling water. She went to the counter to put her hair up which was long and natural. She made a mental note to go to the salon to get her edges trimmed. Her phone alerted a text, so she went to check it. When she opened it, it was a message from Kim saying she was going to have an orgy with Boris Kudjoe and Ryan Gosling.

It was captioned with the image of her and two dildos by her cheeks. Laughing at the photo she responded by calling her a whore, then grabbed her tablet, a small gold cylinder, then went and got into the tub. As she soaked, she would go through her Tuvuler notifications.

She finished, and more were popping up so she told herself she would do the rest later. She sat her tablet to the side and grabbed her gold cylinder which was about 7 inches long and smooth. She placed it under the water and slid right to the tip so it was just at her vagina. She clicked the back and it erupted in vibration. She slowly eased it deeper holding it with both hands grooving her hips on it slowly until she climaxed.

BURBANK CALIFORNIA 1 a.m.

"I will only be gone for 3 days Justine; can we just talk about it when I get back? I would really like to get some sleep. You know I have an early flight."

"Derrick, it's always you want to talk about it when you get back in a couple of hours, a couple of days, or weeks. It's been months now and you act like it's not a big deal."

"Because it's not a big deal. I mean look where I'm at, am I not here?"

"You can physically be somewhere and still not be emotionally there. So yeah for now you are, but what about next week or the week after that. Hell, what about the three days you're about to leave for Derrick? Isn't it ironic how you always have something to do every time I want to talk?"

"No! What's ironic is how every time I need to get something done you want to talk" he snapped back.

"Don't be an asshole it's not your strong suit," she said.

"Not my strong suit... My strong suit? Okay! Let's talk and just get it all out in the open. What is it? I'm all ears" he said sarcastically.

"Do you have to be a smart-ass about it?"

"Just come on I'm tired," he said slapping his hands on his lap.

"Well if you're so tired forget it, it's not important," she said looking away.

"Uggggggghhh" he groaned. "Do you want to talk or not it's simple.

"No, it's not that simple because you're not into this at all and it needs to be taken seriously."

"Justine!" he shouted sitting up placing his back against the headboard. "Let's talk because now I'm getting upset and I don't want to be mean so would you just talk already? I'm up, I'm ready to talk about whatever it is that is going on in your head. Just please let's get on with it."

Justine sat silent scowling at him with daggered eyes.

"Oh, so now you got an attitude?" she asked.

"Goddammit Justine! Do you want to fucking talk or not shit I'm tired of this shit now. Damn it!" he shouted. "Every damn time I come home it's always some shit and when I ask you about it you turn into a fucking deaf-mute."

He was practically screaming, and Justine knew that this would lead to him wanting to drink and leave. It was always like this when she tried to talk to him. He will overreact and storm out which is what she was afraid of. It was also what she wanted to talk about. Every time he stormed out he would drink and sometimes he wouldn't come home. He would stay out all night sometimes for days. She would call but he would only text her back. Yet when he was on his way home he would call her and let her know. He would come back like he knew he was wrong and apologize yet he would never talk about it with her nor discuss where he spent the night. It was the same action she had with her ex-husband. He would do the same when he would cheat on her. It was what he did when she found out that he had another child with another woman.

"This shit is so fucking stupid Justine. Dammit, talk hell I'm up now."

He was putting on his sweatpants and t-shirt. He turned towards her and placed on his sandals.

"Well?!" he said looking at her questionably.

She didn't respond, and he walked out of the bedroom. She found out about the baby and was heartbroken not only because he cheated and had a baby, but also the fact that she couldn't have children. He would get so mad that he would talk down to her and make comments that hurt her heart, comments like "You can't have kids so why should we be married", and "Maybe I should've fucked your friend instead of choosing you the night we met". To make matters worse he beat her in his drunken rages. He would drink, and the rage would lead to him beating her for not being able to give him children, allegations of her cheating, and not supporting him.

When he beat her, it was followed by acts of rape. He would get aroused and fuck her hard in her ass. She would be in tears asking him to stop, but he would just go on until he finished. Leaving her smelling of booze, his sweat, her blood from her anus, and his semen. He would never see it as rape because they were together, but it was to her and it hurt her to her soul.

She finally got enough and as luck would have it her ex-husband left her for another woman. She filed for divorce, and she started over years later when she met Derrick. He was just her type, tall, dark, handsome, funny, financially stable, and well-traveled. As time passed signs started to show and her intuition kicked in and before she knew it the long nights started, then the drinking, then the yelling, so she, just like most women of this type of victimization did...when Derek started to yell... she shut down.

LAW OFFICES OF ROYAL OAKS AND GARDEN 3 p.m.

"**M**s. Frazier your 3 o'clock appointment is here to see you" Kelly said.

"Please send him in Kelly, and thank you"

"Ms. Frazier will see you now Mr. Charles. Right, this way."

Kelly walked the gentleman through the large glass-frosted double doors where Jenna sat prepping for her meeting. She just opened the file to review the fourth time when she saw the silhouette from inside the door. She stood and immediately felt her knees jolt a bit with the hair raising on the back of her neck.

The long fellow strolled towards her in what seemed slow motion as she admired his full lips and strong long jaw. As he approached with his large hand, arm extended, she took him in completely. The smell of musk along with his baritone of a voice made her jolt again. She shook his hand and felt flushed as she could feel her nipples harden.

"My God this man is absolutely gorgeous in person," she thought while doing her research she couldn't believe he was her client. She kicked herself for him being her client. She thought he should be her sexual slave.

"How are you, Mr. Charles? It's a pleasure to meet you." She shook his hand and noticed he didn't have a ring and didn't even have a tan line.

"Please call me Derrick."

"Ok Derrick" motioning for him to have a seat. "How may I help you?"

"You came highly recommended by some friends of mine who raved on and on about your work. Also, you are seen as a rock star in your field so it was a no-brainer that I brought my business to your firm. As I'm sure you know, my company is in a bit of a pickle because of recent disgruntled employees being disrespectful to some clients. I received much backlash from that as well as the numerous claims of sexual harassment allegations from female staff on management. In a nutshell, I need you to help me save my company from the beating in the media we are getting before lawsuits and before I'm faced with my board of directors with a hostile takeover." He paused for a second then said, "I'd also like to take you on a date."

Wow! She thought. Isn't that why his company has sexual harassment suits against it now? Birds of a feather...

She was flattered but needed to set the boundaries immediately. She thanked him for the compliment but said she did not have personal intimate relationships with her clients. Her relationships with her clients were strictly business. She climbed to her position with hard work and not compromising her integrity by sleeping with anyone, client or partner. No matter how attractive she thought he was, he wasn't more attractive than her self-respect. Then, before she knew it she was up on his lap, her blouse open, and her breast out.

He sucked her nipple and she moaned with pleasure as she unhooked his belt and could feel his massive erection through his pants. He lifted her up, sat her on the table, raised her skirt then pulled down her panties. It was purely animalistic. Their passion was so intense struggling attempting to free one leg out of her panties, and he left them hanging off her right ankle. She pulled his pants down just over his knees and started stroking his penis with her right hand. He ached for her as if he would climax at that very moment. She could see it in his eyes that he wanted her urgently. He pulled her close and she took him in her mouth. He almost climaxed instantly leaning back as she sucked him for a few moments. He pulled her to the edge of the table, spread both of her legs apart in the air, kneeled and took her into his mouth. She was throbbing as he French-kissed her clitoris. Her whole body shook for pleasure and her nipples were hard. She placed both hands on his head and pulled him in closer as he sucked and licked her vagina. He stood with her legs still open, wet, and ready. He stroked the head of his penis on her vagina making her pelvis roll. He placed the head in and she felt how full her walls collapsed around him.

"Ms. Frazier! Ms. Frazier!" he called.

"Yes?"

"Are you okay?" he asked looking at her attentively.

"Yes, I'm sorry you were saying?", but she was trying to figure out where she lost the conversation last.

"Are you sure you're okay? We can always reschedule if you aren't feeling well".

"No! No! Not at all. I was just assessing the outcome to foresee the appropriate course of action as there is quite a bit to repair Mr. Charles" she said hopefully in an attempt for recovery.

"Oh okay. Well, as I was saying, I need to control this matter about the sexual harassment claims against my management staff before I lose the position in my company and have to resign".

"I'll be able to handle this effectively Mr. Charles, making you look as if you took the proper actions. I will say the first thing is to consider the immediate suspension of the accused to show not only to employees but also to the public you are taking the matter seriously. It will also build confidence in the victims that your company stands against all improper sexual advancements to its staff and have a zero-tolerance for client mistreatment. This will allow your board members to see you have the matter under control."

As she completed the outline of the appropriate resolution she completed the meeting. He stood satisfied at his choice with her resolve as they were walking out they began to small talk. She agreed to have a drink with him at Pure as he was trying to get on the list. Normally she wouldn't but for her clients, she would.

"So, I'll have a car grab you around 9 p.m.," she told him and he agreed.

Before he exited she asked which friends raved about her and he comically said Google and Wikipedia. He then told her he would see her later that night and left. Smart, handsome, and witty she thought to herself.

TEXT: "I'm sorry about last night. I just wanted to talk, I didn't mean to make you mad. I just want us to be happy. I love you. Can you please call or text me, so I know you made it there safe? I miss you, Derrick."

PURE LOUNGE 9:45 p.m.

D errick, like everyone else, loved the New York nightlife. LA had a beautiful nightlife as well with some of the sexiest people you have ever laid eyes on. Yet New York was still raw, gritty, and primitive. Even the danger of the night had a certain allure of sex appeal. When he heard that Pure was on the east coast, it was something on his bucket list. Everyone out west who had visited the lounge said Robert Louis was just not an app nerd. His ties to the music industry made his awareness of the lounge greater than just a place to go.

It was all a calculated experience. He was detailed even in how he had video from the inside of the lounge outside to make people start to dance in line so they wouldn't get bored and leave. He had the women handpicked from attitude, academic, and physical appearance. The guy even had the bathroom decked out with urinals of what was said to look like beautiful mouths. When Derrick pulled up he was just about to experience all the appeal of Pure Lounge. When the driver opened the door, it looked like a Fashion Week model walk. Beautiful, classy, and strong was everywhere.

The paparazzi was flashing at everything and everyone as he had only been out of the car for 1 minute and saw 10 celebrities. He even found himself recognized as he heard a young photographer yell "Mr. Charles this way!" another said, "Over here Mr. Charles!" and another said, "Derrick look over here!". He knew by 6 a.m. he would find himself in some publication which would make his director call and wonder why he was not handling the matters of the sexual harassment claims and the disgruntled employee. He knew his phone would ring before he even took his morning piss. He also knew they would all kiss his ass as soon as they realized who stood with him in the picture. The new power attorney Jenna Frazier.

Wow! She was hot he thought 5'6 120 lbs. 36-24-36 frame, pearly white smile, flawless skin, and a sex appeal that drew men to her like moths to a flame. He knew she was his shot at the next level for his company's future. He was making his way to the entrance when he saw her coming his way. Man, she was as beautiful as he imagined. Her hair was down and bone straight. She looked exotic even though she was African-American. As a white guy from Mississippi you wouldn't normally be openly attracted to the opposite race yet this wasn't the 50s or 60s and he wasn't in Mississippi nor did he give a shit. She had curves that screamed at him. She approached, took his arm in hers, and she gave him the most beautiful smile. She was a pleasurable toxin of chemistry no doubt with a trail of men still crying over her from letting her go or not trying at all.

"Ms. Frazier," he said

"Mr. Charles, this way" she grabbed him by the arm and the cameras flashed away. (Music playing Boom... Boom... Clap... Boom... Boom...Clap! Hello! Good morning!) P Diddys Dirty Money hit "Hello, Good Morning" boomed through the lounge. It seemed like it was in the queue to play when Derrick and Jenna walked in the door. It looked like The Tunnel back in the 90s how the dance floor was packed with cocktail dresses and suits of high fashion grooving.

It looked like a music video during flash scenes. P Diddy wasn't there in person, but his energy was and you knew why he was one of the world's top music moguls. "Wow," Derrick thought to himself as a 5'11 blonde with legs for days escorted them to the VIP Section where a good amount of celebs were but it was center lounge for Derrick and Jenna. Once seated they were approached by another server who bought a bottle of Victor O'Neill Cognac and Winecoff Vodka, soda, cranberry, and orange juice.

"What's this?" Derek asked.

"Compliments of Mr. Louis," the pretty brunette said as she sat down the glasses. "These are the new brands of spirits the owner will be launching soon so you two are getting an exclusive taste test for this evening. Which would you like to start with? Let me guess you're a vodka guy, right?" she said smiling.

"That Mr. Louis does his homework doesn't he?" Derrick said feeling all the senses of this being pre-arranged and methodically thought out.

Jenna looked at him and gave a confident head nod.

"I heard about this place but man it didn't do justice at all. This is incredible".

As Derek spoke Jenna was taking him in again knowing what he was experiencing as she did when she first came. She always got that feeling when she came to Pure.

"How about some shots," she said grabbing the vodka.

"Oh, you're my kind of lawyer Ms. Frazier".

She poured what looked like a double shot for them both, handed him a glass, then toasted to bright futures. He tapped her glass and watched her take the whole shot at once. "Oh man she is awesome," he thought. He did the same.

"Oh, this is good," she said.

"I agree. It has the right kind of punch to it."

She poured them another but allowed them to sit for a second. If she remembered correctly the bartenders would prefer to serve hard drinks in 20-minute intervals to minimize the prompt of intoxication. Too much too fast would cause them to ask the patron to stop drinking. Plus, she didn't want to get wasted in front of a client as it wasn't professional nor was it ladylike.

"So, do you always work or do you have a personal life you getaway to?" he asked.

"Personal life?" she looked at him with a shocked expression. "Is that what they call always working, dream about vacations you never take, but spend all your money on bills and lending to family members that never pay you back?"

"Wait, no. That's the definition of responsibility" he said.

"No that's the ingredients on the back of vinegar jars," she said.

"I hate vinegar," he said.

She grabbed her shot and handed him his and toasted to hating vinegar. They talked more a bit and Derrick asked her if she wanted to dance. She looked at him as if he was crazy.

"Can you dance?" she asked.

He smiled "Come and see".

She conceded and hit the dance floor as Maroon 5 carried the crowd into a rhythmic wave. He was a towering presence, but he had moves for a white guy.

He leaned in and said "I have some moves for a white guy. Justin Timberlake ain't got nothing on me."

"Justin Timberlake?" she said.

He said, "Yeah Justin Timberlake".

She tapped his chest and pointed at the stage when all of a sudden, the crowd went insane. The lead and acoustic guitar broke into a rhythm and he went into his hit song "Not a Bad Thing". "Oh, this is a good day," she thought. They danced close and sang the words with Justin. He spun her around placing her back against his chest in a standing spooning position. They danced that way for the complete song occasionally making eye contact. He whispered something in her ear and it seemed to stun her for a second, then she looked at him over her right shoulder. He had his arms around her waist and she had hers over him. She nodded, and they made their way off the dance floor, grabbed their things from VIP, and headed to the door. They left in the same black town car.

EAST VILLAGE BROWNSTONE 2 a.m.
(1 YEAR LATER)

B uzz! Buzz!...Buzz! Buzz!
"Derrick your phone is going off again."

Buzz! Buzz!...Buzz! Buzz!

"Derrick!" Jenna turned the light on.

"Hmmm?" He mumbled.

"Your phone is going off again... At 2 a.m. of all times." she sat up looking at his side of the bed.

He rolled over to get his phone. It was notifications from his email. "It's just emails coming through."

"Emails?"

"Yes... Emails."

"Who emails at 2 a.m.?!"

"I don't know... We do."

"What do you mean we do? I'm not emailing anyone at 2 a.m. What are you talking about?"

Derrick just rolled over and grunted. "Turn off the light Jenna please."

"I'm just saying Derrick your phone goes off all times of night, and the whole thing with Justine just has me on edge. So, don't try to play it like it's nothing" she said with the light on.

"Do we have to go through this now?" he asked with his back turned to her.

"No, we don't have to go through it now, but at some point, we have to properly address it okay?" she said to the back of his head feeling disrespected.

"Okay, I promise we will, now will you turn off the light?"

If he would have seen her face he would have seen that she was near slapping his head. She nodded and said, "okay".

She laid down and was fuming. She was barely calming down when the phone went off again.

Buzz!...Buzz!

"Derrick!" she screamed.

"What?!"

"Your phone that's what. Turn it off at least give me that respect."

"Aggh I swear."

"You swear what Derrick? You swear what? My phone isn't the one going off in the middle of the damn night. You know what? I'm going to sleep in the spare bedroom."

She got up and took her housecoat as he was still lying on the bed when the door slammed. She laid down in the spare bedroom with tears in her eyes. She knew she wasn't crazy. Something was going on, but she didn't want to admit it. She couldn't help her intuition. It screamed at her. She saw his phone had a message from Justine, and even though she didn't read the whole thing, enough was on it for her to see that Justine was involved with him intimately to some degree.

He told her it wasn't what she thought but something told her it was everything she thought. Justine, then Erica, his friend Keisha, and God knows who else. He said it was just business but no woman contacts a man at all hours of the night knowing he is in a relationship. No woman references a man talking about "Things between us", and is still talking about business. He was everything she wanted, and she was successful as well. They made the perfect couple, and he was her type so what changed that made the dynamic between them cold? That night after the lounge was amazing. She wouldn't normally go for a client, but Derrick was perfect for her, and there was nothing in the policy saying it wasn't allowed.

Morally, it was looked down upon, but the partners would see it her way since she was doing so well, and it didn't affect her work because she did save his company and him as she said she would. She cried herself to sleep. In the other room, Derrick picked up his phone and saw the emails from the dating site he had been on for years now. He met so many women on the site he was always going on dates in different cities. The women were top-notch model types who were nothing less of arm candy and Derrick had a major sweet tooth. This week alone he already slept with two women from the site.

He was having fun plus he knew women just wanted money. They didn't care much about love or relationships so why should he? Why settle down? He thought. Dating is more fun, and although Jenna was hot, so was all the other ones. He hadn't intended for her to get serious, but it just did. It was time he cut the cord with them and head back to LA. He would settle down one day just not today he thought. Tomorrow he and Jenna would just have to break up simple as that.

Justine sat outside the brownstone staring at the window. Her heart was pounding, and she was furious.

How could he do this to her? He lied for so long and all she wanted was for them to work things out. He said she was his lawyer, but the tabloids said differently.

When she asked him about the relationship he denied it. He didn't know she had had them followed. When she called him earlier he told her he was running late and called her by the wrong name. He tried to act like it was a mistake and it was. It was his last mistake he would ever make. She reached into her purse and pulled out the nickel-plated Derringer. She made sure it was loaded. She took a long swig from the flask s, placed the lid on the flask, sat it on the passenger seat, and got out of the car. She looked to her left, then to her right. The street being empty she had almost contemplated getting back in the car and going back to LA. She looked up and down the street again and she walked up to the brownstone door.

REASON TWO

HE'S AN OPPORTUNIST

Somewhere in the world right now there's a female who has a talent that she is hoping will take her to the next level. I'm using the term talent loosely because it can refer to all types of industries. Legal, music, food service, travel, etc. You could even use the word skill, but I want to shed light on two age-old industries which are tv and music. She always wanted to be a singer or an actress since she was just a little kid. She grew up to be quite the looker who honed her skills to get to the right kinds of people who could take her to the next level. She did her research and she knows just the direction she wants to go.

So, one day while out and about, at a networking event, she meets a guy who seems to appeal to all of her interests. He seems to be famous as the people in the room acknowledge his presence happily and he seems to fit with her ambitions. They decide to switch numbers and in a matter of weeks they are dating. He is now helping her with her career. He introduces her to some new business associates, and now work for her seems to be a good amount to launch her career. She has allowed this guy into her life as well as into her body because he seems to have her best interest at heart. Then one day she starts to notice how he directs his attention to another "her". Not her twin, but someone he could help succeed the same. She is everything she is just a newer version and is about to experience the same fate...She, my dear will do all the normal "whys" that come along, and she will receive all the same "becauses".

Guys who cheat like this feed off women's ambitions to be independent successful women and it has been happening since the beginning of all industries involving women. Hell, women do it too but not as much as men. Why? I don't know. Well, I could explain it, but that would take more elaboration and dilute the raw truth regarding this simple, and direct approach that just gets to the point. You know the saying "when opportunity knocks you should answer". Well the next time you come across a guy and he seems like he has all the answers to your ambitious needs, you may want to tell him to go fuck himself...but be a lady about it.

Mr. Opportunity uses this approach to not only succeed where he would normally fail at getting women of his desire to have sex with him, but he also uses this tactic to cash in. One second, she's meeting people he says she will need to make it, then some dinners, drinks, and some failed leads later she will be having sex with him because she is convinced the two will be the next Sara Jessica Parker/Mathew Broderick, Jay-Z/Beyoncé, Tom Hanks/Rita Wilson, and RV/Lillie Mae. Then he will need to borrow x amount of dollars because it's going to help her get to this other person or pay for that. By the time the smoke clears she's broke, about to be homeless, and shit she just might be pregnant.

THE QUEEN

"Big party tonight. There will be some important people in attendance that you will be meeting so bring your 'A' game. Smile. Will be at your place at 8 to get you" -BC

"Okay. I will be ready. I'll finish up at the shop as fast as I can. Have you heard anything else about Queen? Figured they would say something by now" -KR

"LMAO! It's only been 3 days Kimmie they will call I promise. They are my peeps so they will lookout. Let's focus on now okay?" -BC

"All right! But you will let me know when they call back right?" -KR

"Of course! Of course! But we may want to get some more classes though just to put you in a better place. I can get you a good deal with someone that is A list" -BC

"Huh? Acting classes? How much? I've put a lot into this already and I don't have much in my savings" -KR

"I know Kimmie but this is what it takes and I put a good deal into getting you to this point and you see where we are. It's a good bit but I will meet you halfway so it won't be a total hit for you okay? Trust me it will be good and I wouldn't say it if it wasn't" -BC

"I know and I do appreciate you for everything. How much, and I will get it together. Just have to move some things around but I will make it work" -KR

"BC? You there? Hello?" -KR

"Yeah" -BC

"Thought I lost you did you get my last text?" -KR

"Yeah. In the middle of a meeting. Will call you after okay? Don't forget about tonight." -BC

"Wait how much do I need for the class so I can go by the bank?"-KR

"$3,000" -BC

"$3,000! Shit! That's about all I have BC" -KR

"I said I would do half but if you can't swing it I'll get it. Just trying to lock you in. Wouldn't want you to lose an opportunity on a technicality you know. It happens, Kimmie. It's New York they sleep acting here. Real acting" -BC

"I know I just wasn't prepared for that number. If it helps I will do it. I'll leave now and get it" -KR

"Good deal. I will see you tonight...Will drop by, grab that since it's on the way then I will meet you later tonight" -BC

"Okay have a good meeting" -KR

;-) -BC

TAYLOR ACTING 2 MONTHS LATER

"Okay great session today class you all were amazing. Give yourselves a round of applause. Today is a bittersweet moment as one of our own Kimberly Reynolds will be leaving us for the big screen."

The whole class looked at her with somber envious smiles, and she looked at them all with a "Thank you fuck you bitches!" expression along with her "I can't wait to leave here" smile.

"Hopefully Ms. Reynolds will not forget about us and drop in on us whenever she has the time. Let's give her a round of applause."

Everyone clapped as she thought "Not in a million years you disgusting prick". Yet BC was right about her taking the class. The director hadn't made up his mind about her having the part. She knew she was right for it and had everything they were looking for, but he was stalling. It seemed BC had her going all around town meeting people, shaking the right hands, being in all the right places. Something was still missing so when she attended the acting class she ended up going back in front of the director again. This time she really wowed him. At any moment she thought she was sure he was going to call with the final decision to use her.

It had been six weeks that passed since the night he invited her to dinner. At first, she didn't think anything about it, but when she agreed to a nightcap she saw what he wanted. Against her better judgment, she slept with him anyway. She cried the whole time in the shower when she got home. She tried her best to scrub the guilt of sleeping with a director off to confirm her role, but it was too deep. She did get the part although her actions would not allow her to enjoy it inside. Outside she was becoming the center of attention. All the news, blogs, radio, and social media outlets were raving about her. She was about to launch a career as an actress with the whole world knowing her name. She allowed herself to feel accomplished. Her phone rang, and the screen said BC. She answered.

"Hello BC"

"Hello BC? You mean hello God after all I've done for you honey you should call me Almighty."

"I will do no such thing that's blasphemy BC you know we southerners take religion seriously."

"Well how about Jesus, Mother Teresa" he said jokingly.

"Not even the son" she responded.

"Well, what would you call me after the heavenly results of all of my hard work with you getting the biggest role in the "it" movie to watch?"

"I'd call you well-compensated after your percentages you weasel."

"Weasel? How dare you call me a weasel you, dork, you'll thank me when you win an Oscar."

"If I win an Oscar I'll have your baby BC" she laughed.

"Oh, the hell you will my little shining star I wouldn't dare have another me on this God-awful planet. Too much bureaucracy and the world is going to hell."

"So why are you in the business if you don't like bureaucracy and the world is going to hell?"

"Because my shining star... I have expensive taste and I can't buy my luxuries acting all moral and shit so whatever. The lawyers are going over your contract and it should be finalized by the morning. Do you have any other requests or addendums before it's completed?"

"No. It was all covered when I checked it the last time so I'm ready to go. I heard we are going on location as soon as the ink dries."

"You heard right my dear. I must say that Terrence Khavi is a pusher pusher pusher but you would know all about that wouldn't you?" BC said.

"What are you talking about BC?"

"Nothing! I'm not implying nothing at all, but you are the new taste of the month so don't act as if you aren't indulging and knowing Mr. Director is calling you his sweetheart."

"Where did you hear that?"

"I read it in Variety goodness stop at the newsstand why don't you."

Had she committed and not known? This celeb spin on life and relationships was already taking on its own form with her. Something she didn't want to yield to. Yet it wouldn't be so bad to be openly wanted by Khavi, to have the whole world fondle over her, have guys in prison masturbating to her pictures, have young girls wanting to dress like her, and wanting to be like her. She wanted to be famous, so she could show everyone who doubted her, she made it. Kim from Kannapolis made it, and maybe when the world saw her in the spotlight she would finally feel accepted by The Who's Who of the world.

She would be equal in success besides her best friend Jenna who she loved so much. Jenna had been there for her through thick and thin. Even on the night that her dad left her and her mom. Even though she was only 8 years old she remembered how empty she felt. She still didn't know why, but she knew that she loved her dad. Her mom and dad would argue a lot, and there were moments when she saw her dad grab her mom, but her mom broke free and shut the door that night. She couldn't see but she heard strange noises coming from her parents' bedroom.

Thumps, crashes, and claps. She kept hearing the claps and her mom making scream like noises. She would run in her room and shut the door to hide under her covers with her favorite stuffed animal which was a star with a smiley face. Her Grandpa gave it to her because he said she would be a star one day just like the people on TV. That night she got up from the front door shutting. Her dad was leaving when she looked out the window. She went to her parents' room where her mom was lying on the floor. She could see her feet from beside the bed. She walked in saying "mama" but her mom did not answer her. She walked closer and called her mom again, but her mom did not answer. She walked all the way over to the side of the bed where her mother laid.

Her face was covered in purple and blood badly swollen. "Mommy!" She began to cry. Her mom made a slight moan and raised her shaking arm to Kim. Kim kneeled to lay beside her cradled in her mom's arm around her crying until she fell asleep. Jenna came to sleep over just hours later as she was running late. Their families knew each other so Jenna just ran into the house with her mom just behind her. Jenna searched for Kim until she saw her in her parents' room and screamed so loud it woke Kim. Jenna's mom rushed to the room and nearly fainted at what she saw. She quickly told Jenna to call 911. She checked Kim's mom's vitals but there was no need. She died with her daughter in her arms.

"You are not just the hottest actress out you have a royal relationship, my dear... Gosh, you're going to make me indispensable."

"Oh my God BC seriously?!" she said sarcastically.

"Yes," he said surely.

"Well, I guess we cannot keep the world waiting can we. I need to call Jenna and tell her the news." He cut her off.

"Later. I need you to do a couple of interviews right now, and right after we have to be over at Conde Nash"

"Huh?" she said shocked. A black limo pulled up to a stop in front of her. The driver stepped out, the back window rolled down, and BC's face emerged still on the phone.

"Out with the old in with the new," he said. She smiled and got in.

CABO SAN LUCAS, MEXICO

Knock! Knock! "Yes!" Kim's voice called from inside the trailer.

The D.A. opened the door and said: "10 minutes to set Ms. Reynolds".

"Okay thank you," she said while her makeup was being completed.

She sat viewing herself as "The Queen", a role for one of the most notorious female drug lords in South America. Shooting in Cabo San Lucas by the beach, she and the rest of the crew took it all in as it felt more like a vacation instead of work. Terrance and she made a bet; the winner got the location of choice as they couldn't openly decide. She won, but it felt like everyone won. Matter-of-factly she and Terrance were actually more serious than she expected. He wasn't all Hollywood as she first figured. He was actually just like her in many ways. He worked hard in theater and set out to make a movie from a play he directed.

The play took off and now he was a hotshot movie director whom you could say earned his way to the top. They appeared at all the go-to spots for the famous on most nights. She thought it was only for a publicity stunt at first. When they talked about their past she could feel he had genuinely taken to her. So, she decided not only to commit to the feeling of their union but allowed him to enter her without a condom...a decision she was fearing lately that may change her life. The thought alone made her place her hand over her stomach.

TWO WEEKS LATER, 5 A.M.

The hustles and bustle of New York was in full swing on Sunday morning even in the snow. Construction workers were hammering away on scalpels as the sun was breaking. You would consider this method as to how America was built... well in New York anyway. In the South not even, the rooster crowed on Sunday morning. Even the rooster knew it was God's day and knew to just sleep in. However New Yorkers seem to never know this or acknowledge it and felt it was good as any day to show the world why it was more productive than anywhere else. How could you sleep with so much money to be made? That to New Yorkers is just a mystery.

The world continued to sleep while Kim and New York were at it. She stood looking out of the window in downtown Brooklyn at the Indigo Hotel, between Albee Square W and Duffield St. She could see the Macy's store across the street. Later, just below a couple of blocks, she would be receiving her dinner from Juniors. She ordered breakfast from room service. The Indigo was her local hideaway as she tried to get her life back together. At least she could try to figure it all out. How did she get to this point she asked herself? She went from the most wanted woman in America to... now the cast out, disgruntled, abandoned girl who just got dropped by her boyfriend, the movie, and America it seems... 'That bitch!' seemed to be the only thing she could muster out of her mouth. How long had she been working that angle, and how come she did not pick it up?

The news came at the worst timing of her life, scarring it with tainted memory. She had this elaborate plan together by announcing it on the Good Morning America daytime show. She showed the ultrasound letting the world know she and Khavi were expecting a baby and it wouldn't interrupt the movie. It was going to be perfect. The world knew and so many fans are even trying to name the baby for her. She even thought of naming the baby after her mom if it was a girl.

She started shopping for the baby's room, anticipating the baby shower, but more importantly giving the baby a childhood better than she had. All that would be just wishful thinking for the most part because she was off the movie, BC dropped her, and she no longer knew how she would afford the lifestyle. She felt ashamed to ask for money from her friends as she knew she could, but her pride wouldn't allow her. She wasn't returning phone calls or messages.

Reporters and different gossip magazines wanted her side of the story. She knew they would have her on the front pregnant, in shades, looking depressed with some degrading title like, "Out of Hollywood, Out of Work, Out of Hope for the Baby" or "Baby May Go to Adoption", or "Drug Abuse Reason for Loss of Part in Movie". Life as she seemed to know it would cease to exist in the happy realm she originally thought. She felt she may end up working some dead-end job now just to make it...may go back to Kannapolis just to find someone who may still find her worthy of dating.

Khavi wasn't even responding to her calls anymore. He even told her he wasn't sure if the baby was his. He hurt her to her core. She knew she could get the DNA test but the mere fact he denied it was just overbearing. She wished she could talk to her mom, she wished she could even talk to Jenna, but neither one of them were available for her to talk with. Looking out as the men of New York continued to hammer and weld away she reached into her purse for her cell phone.

When she turned on the phone it chimed with alerts from emails, voicemails, texts, and Tuvuler messages. Once the notification for all the missed phone calls stopped, she scrolled her contacts for someone who could provide temporary relief. She told herself this will be the last time because of the baby. She will not get high again. The phone rang once before the man's voice said,

"I knew you would be calling me. I've been waiting for you. Where are you?"

"Brooklyn, Indigo Hotel, downtown."

He said he would be there in 20 minutes.

She hung up the phone and reached in her purse for her black compact case. She opened it viewing the last remains of the powder. The last time she thought again to herself. Grabbing a small pic with an oval tip that looked like a micro-spoon, she scooped the powder then sniffed it hard into her nose. She began to take her clothes off as when the guy arrives she knew how he would want to see her. She knew how he would want her too. Sitting in the chair she took another spoonful of powder and sniffed it. Then she waited.

MONDAY 9:27 A.M.

Camera snaps shots of a man leaving the Indigo Hotel in a hurry

REASON 3

HE'S A MANDINGO

As somewhat self-explanatory, the title directs this reason like all the others. It's an exact focal point of character mentality. Outside of Mandingo being an African tribe, during the conditioning of slavery where the Mandingo is greatly exhibited, slave conditioning could only prevail with actual slaves. Although it was an abomination, slave conditioning was more successful not by the actual taking of slaves, but in the breeding of slaves.

Slave creators, the originators of the "Mandingo" personality or act, realized if they made a slave from birth they would be more obedient, and less likely to run off, unlike the ones they had to capture and beat senselessly into slavery. This caused many slaves prospects injury, sickness, and some even death.

So, to preserve their stock, slave creators would find male slaves who had large penises to have sex to get female slaves pregnant. Well, not all day, just to breed with. Once babies were born they were nursed, many not by their own mothers. Some would be sold and some kept...even the ones the slave creators had with the slave women who had lesser melanin in skin complexion. This means lighter skin for you who don't know how skin pigmentation is gauged. Those with lighter skin would be used more so in the house.

The Mandingo slave was only to have sex and provide no other obligation or emotional attachment to the woman or the child. Doing so could cost him his life. The Mandingo has evolved greatly to present society. Some women like Mandingo and some can't take the Mandingo. When you meet the Mandingo, his mind has been made up for decades and not even you can really change him. His goal is to have sex and well...more sex. He will take it whenever it becomes available from you, your friend, your neighbor, the girl at the gym, women from work, the pretty lady at the grocery store, and most definitely the celebrity he has had a crush on. It just doesn't matter.

There are Mandingos of all ethnic groups too, so you can't just isolate them to the one described. He probably has more options than TDH but less than CC.

Today, the Mandingo has a lot of help to keep him cheating on you as well. Two of the reasons are those that actually helped create him. His large penis, and women who like men with large penises. A woman who has a guy with a below-average less than 6in. penis will less likely be hassled than a guy who may have a larger 8in. penis. As long as she is getting the climax that she doesn't get at home, some women are not concerned if he's in a relationship or not. The Mandingo is very familiar with this scenario, so he builds his whole lifestyle around it. This is his method of attracting more women.

By the time you meet Mandingo and feel as if you hit the bedroom lottery, Mandingo is only fulfilling his unconscious conditional genetic duty until he comes across another candidate to recycle the act. So, before you consider yourself solely interested in a guy that has to have a big penis, consider not only the traffic on it but as well as its commitment to its history. Kind of hard to tell a child his father is not around because he couldn't keep his penis in his pants when that was the reason you wanted him in the first place. Bow chicka wow wow.

INDECENT FORGIVENESS HARKER HEIGHTS TEXAS JUNE 2001

———————

Summer in Texas is a beautiful season for the Longhorn State. It means some of the most beautiful of God's creations walking around in cut off shorts, tank tops, and cowboy boots. It means that the fire department would also be at local high school football fields to spray them down, so they wouldn't overheat. It means that the heat index could be tested by dropping an egg on the concrete to make breakfast. It means Harleys, Suzuki's, and other similar bikes will be occupants of the long roads through Austin, Round Rock, and San Antonio for evening getaways from the inner cities.

It would also mean most of the soldiers at the near Fort Hood military base, in Killeen Texas, the largest installation in the world, would be buzzing with hundreds of thousands of US servicemen and women training to keep our United States safe. The men and women of our United States armed forces are the absolute best at what they do and are the pride of America's heartbeat. Yet the Texas Summer is also notorious for some of love's worst heartbreaks. Heartbreaks that might change people's lives forever. The type of heartbreak that takes a life.

Robert Louis had only been in Texas to visit his fiancé Camille Scott when he decided he would move from North Carolina to be closer to her. He told only his grandparents who weren't completely happy to see him leave but they understood the situation. His boss at the shoe store he worked for was able to get him transferred to the Texas location in the Killeen Mall just off of highway 14. This decision seemed like the right thing to do since his last visit went so well after spending only 3 days in the military town.

He saved up enough money to go and surprise Camille while she was in basic training at Fort Jackson South Carolina then sent off for AIT phase IV and V training in Virginia before joining their unit. Showing up on the Fort Hood base in a limo with a dozen long stem red roses, he waited behind a large group of soldiers standing in formation. When called over to the limo, Camille was in complete shock when she saw him. The reaction of the other soldiers was the same, seeing that PFC Scott was associated with such a successful guy. At least on the surface.

They had such an amazing time for those 3 days of sightseeing and lovemaking. They talked about it and he had made up his mind that he will come around the time she would go for NTC training in California. By the time she got back, he would be set up and she would move in with him to an apartment off base. He arrived in Texas renting a one-bedroom one-bathroom apartment in Lookout Ridge Apartments just behind Winn-Dixie grocery store and Cactus Cannon Bar and Grill. It was nice, affordable, and occupied by both military personnel and civilians.

Camille had just bought her greens and other issued items, so she would have them when she returned from training. Robert had yet to get bedroom furniture. All he had was a living room suite from Rent-A-Center with dishes, TV, radio, and groceries. It was only him for the next two weeks, so he figured he would just make a cot of blankets he had on the floor but after two nights he just slept on the couch.

One day while cleaning out the closet Camille's Army duffle bag fell and a note from a guy named Brandon fell out the head. The note was thanking her for a great night and to make plans to see her again. He placed the letter back and tried not to think about it. He couldn't shake the feeling he got with Camille from previous times. Like the time when she was at a club in Charlotte North Carolina and called him to come pick her and some friends because someone flattened her tires.

71

It was 3 a.m. when he showed up seeing her with one female friend, the rest being two guys. Believing they were just friends he took them all home. It was later in his life he would find out what really happened that night. He also had the same feeling when Camille was alone with his friend who was ex-military. He just knew something happened but couldn't confirm it.

When Camille called from California she told him Brandon was a friend when he inquired about the note. She said he came on to her, but she told Brandon she was in a relationship and they could be nothing more. She told him she and Brandon only really associated because they were in the same platoon something Robert could only respect. It was common for platoon members to bond as in times of battle they would only have each other to watch each other's backs in life-threatening situations. He was well aware of how someone could develop intimate feelings given those circumstances.

Robert was deeply in love with Camille, he would have done anything for her so like all other times he believed her. When Camille returned from NTC in California they spent the evening over dinner and much lovemaking. They were extremely sexually compatible and often went at it like crazed maniacs. It was one of the reasons he was into her. She challenged him in the bedroom and he humbly accepted. When Camille returned life was good, and good was big, about as good could get in Texas life. Yet Texas did big bad as well... Really well.

July 2004 KANNAPOLIS NORTH CAROLINA

———

Magnolia Apartments was a townhouse community about a mile down into Shady Lane in Kannapolis that had a one-way entrance and a one-way out exit. Though the townhouses themselves were brand new, it was here where Robert would often visit his childhood friend Romello Green. Romello was also the cousin of Jasmin Green who was Camille Scott's best friend.

When Robert proposed to Camille, Jasmin was there to sing a Brian McKnight song called "I've Never Felt This Way", but when the time came and the ring arrived in the dessert at Applebee's she was so emotional, she cried so hard she couldn't sing the song. Now back from Texas he would go by and say hello to Jasmin. They both grew up in the same neighborhood as Kim, Romello, Tariq, Jenna, Ros, Mack, Tony, Thomas, Lil Chris, Michael, and the others.

Jasmin was divorced from Kirk and had a son from their marriage. She now lived alone with him and gained a considerable amount of weight. She sent a message back to Robert that she needed to talk to him and it was very important. Anyone who knew him knew that when his friends called on him he always showed up and that's one characteristic they loved about him. He pulled up to the townhouse, got out and knocked on the door. She answered the door in a Carolina blue t-shirt and jeans. Even though she gained some weight Jasmin still was an attractive woman who carried herself well.

"What's up Fatboy, how you doing?"

"What's up Jas? What's so important that you had me rushing down here for?" he asked.

"Come on in and I'll explain everything."

He walked in and she shut the door behind him. Instead of wasting a lot of time she jumped right into her reason for getting him to come by. It had also been the reason he looked at her as if she had shocked his life all over again. The facial expression was only a reminder of the scar he bore across his heart. Even the mention of the name almost gave him an anxiety attack.

"What did you just say?"

"I said Camille wants to have dinner with you."

"For what?"

"She wants to get back with you."

"You have got to be kidding me Jas."

"No kidding, as a matter of fact, she offered me $100 if I could get you to go to dinner."

Almost smiling, deep down inside he always knew she'd realize she made a big mistake and come back. Yet the cut was too deep, and it was beyond repair. Nothing on the planet would get him back to her.

"Fuck no!"

"Fatboy come on."

"Hell, no Jas not in a million years, not for a million dollars, and a million Super Bowl tickets."

"It's just dinner it ain't like you going to marry the..." she stopped and looked away saddened by what she just said. She could feel the pain burning through her and she could barely look at him.

In a low painful voice, he said: "I can't Jas, I just can't." She looked at her longtime friend seeing him almost relive the damage her other longtime friend done to him. Fatboy always was nice to her like all the others they grew up with. He was more like a brother than a friend and would do anything for them. It almost broke her heart to see him this way, yet Camille was her friend too, plus Camille had done a terrible thing which led to something even more tragic. Yet Jasmin thought that maybe time healed those wounds and this could get them back to a good place.

"Fat boy listen" calling him by his childhood name, "Camille knows she made a grave mistake and she has beaten herself up about it for a very long time."

"So?"

"So, I think you should hear her out." She regretted it before it all came out of her mouth. He snapped.

"I should hear her out? Really? Why the fuck should I hear her out Jas? It's not my fault we didn't last."

He was fuming and Jasmin didn't want to dig deeper, but she promised Camille she would get him to have dinner with her. She thought for a second and knew she had some leverage...she just hoped it would work.

"You need this to close the door Fat," she said looking into his eyes grabbing his hand.

He was about to speak but he didn't. He just looked at her credibly.

"I don't think you ever got your answers for why and looking at you now I can tell you could benefit from the closure."

He just stared at her. She looked at him, then her eyes darted as to keep talking, as he may go for it.

"Look, Camille went through her own hell too and it would be good for you to hear it."

He leaned back into the sofa.

"I don't want to say it all because she needs to tell you but it's something you may want to hear," she said hoping this really got him on the hook.

She wanted to have the dinner promise kept to Camille and she did want him to have the closure, yet she also wanted that $100 because Kurt wasn't paying child support, and she could use all the money she could get...even if it meant trying to play matchmaker. He said quietly looking at his hometown childhood friend.

They were both quiet then he spoke "Okay".

She didn't respond as she knew from his expression there would be more.

"I'll do it just so you can get the money, but you also have to stay for dinner and she has to pay."

"She said she would pay for the dinner, but okay I will tell her."

"No call her and tell her now."

She grabbed the phone and dialed the number. He was in close range, so he heard the whole conversation. He heard the voice he had once loved so much...hearing how excited she was and agreeing to be present for the dinner. Once the call was over she told him they would meet at Julian's in Concord Mills Mall at 8 p.m. on Friday. A lot changed since they saw each other. One thing more noticeable for Robert was that he has completely transformed. His hair was cut into deep waves, and his body was that of a football player. He had done okay for himself as most knew because he was doing well in the music industry for a guy starting out. He was attractive. When he left Jasmin's house he almost wanted to tell her he changed his mind and wouldn't go yet he cranked up his Mazda 626 and drove off.

FRIDAY NIGHT 8 p.m. JILLIAN'S JULY 2004

―――

"What am I doing here?" Robert thought sitting in the parking lot. Jillians was a place he would frequent with his brother Michael, Tariq, Romello and Walter. It had a nightclub attached to it that opened around 11 p.m. when the mall closed. It had a bar, DJ booth, and two cages where women would dance. It only filled a couple of hundred people, but it was a nice watering hole for them. Around this time, it was busy with shoppers, teenagers in the game room, and people at the bar...some were even at the bowling alley. He figured he already promised so he might as well get it over with.

Plus, Jas was right, he did want the closure. He wanted to know why she let him move halfway across the US to get his heartbroken. He wanted her to let him know why she abandoned him. He took a deep breath and walked into Jillian's. Jasmin just called his cell phone when he got in the door. She told him where they were sitting, and he saw them. She was just as he remembered her. She gained some weight but she still had that girl next door look. Camille had always been attractive. As he approached the table he smiled at Jas with a slight nod of acknowledgment and did the same with Camille.

Camille rose to give him a hug and as she just got in reach his 9mm exploded into her chest. The shock of the crowd had yet to reach fear when her eyes wide open, arms out like wings, fell backward on the table. The blood-splatter spread all over Jasmin's face and into her eyes. Her mouth dropped open as she saw her best friend lying dead spilling water and glass all over the table.

The customers were all running for the exits in panic and someone yelled "Call 911!". She looked at Robert in chaotic fear as he stood expressionless over Camille's lifeless body. He stepped closer, lifted his 9mm again and squeezed three more rounds in her head...Bang!...Bang!...Knock! "Fatboy," Jasmin said, outside of his window.

He looked at her and rolled it down "Huh?"

"Are you okay?"

"Yes, I'm good. What's up?"

"Not much, I just got here, and she is already inside. Are you ready?"

Taking a deep breath, he said: "Yes let's get this over with."

Wearing makeup that looked almost natural, 21 lbs. heavier guessing around 145lbs now, short haircut, and a slight 40ish spread, Camille looked exactly the same if not better. They seated, ordered drinks, and Jas left them to talk which seemed too long-awaited.

"I was stupid Robert. I was stupid, and I never should have hurt you. After everything happened I wondered what happened to you. No one heard or saw you. Where did you go?"

"I stayed in Texas...moved out to San Marcos to attend Texas State University. I used school to distract the way I truly felt. I was running from all that happened, so it worked out because no one knew me. I was too embarrassed to go home."

"I see," she said, sitting back.

"Why am I here Camille?" he asked sternly.

"I...I wanted to see you, Robert. I needed to say I'm sorry. You were great to me and I blew it with us. I was hoping you would give me another chance."

"Why in the hell would I do that?"

"Because you...I've changed."

"Good for you I hope that change is working for you, but hell will freeze over before I am with you again."

"I know I hurt you and I can't take it back but all I can do is show you that I have changed."

"You don't need to show me anything Camille I'm good and I've moved on just like you did," he said. You were with Brandon last I heard from Phillip so what happened to that?"

Jas looked at Camille and Camille looked as if she wanted to run out of there. She looked back at Robert misty-eyed.

"He left me. He left me with a daughter and moved back to New York to be with his ex."

The blood in his veins boiled all the way to the brink of eruption. His tone was cold ice cold.

"You mean you cheated on me with a guy who left you with the baby after you knew I wanted children with you?"

The room seems to spin and cloud to black.

HARKER HEIGHTS 2001

"**Y**ou were amazing last night" Robert said looking at Camille. She was coming out of the shower.

"You were good too. Lord knows I needed that."

'We're going to do it tonight as well" he said smiling.

"Why wait for tonight?" she dropped her towel exposing her light caramel skin, perky C cup breast, and freshly shaven vagina. She walked over to him and mounted him. They kissed and made love for the second time.

"I have to be at work by 11 a.m. I will be there until about the same time tonight but will try to get out of the store early" he said brushing his teeth.

Camille was dressed standing in the door of the small bathroom wearing his Iceberg shirt. "I'm going to get my hair done but I will stop by when I'm finished."

"Okay cool"

She kissed him and she left into the living room. He arrived at the mall about 10:30 a.m. that morning and Valley the store manager was waiting.

"Hello Valley."

"Gewt mornin Wobert" she responded with her heavy German accent. "Sorry to have you come in but I need to run around wit my guls, and wit Janet out, I don't know what else to do. Janet said she may come in, but I don't know you know?"

"I know Valley. It's okay I got it."

"Here are the keys it's been slow but may pick up later. Nadia and Emmanuel, the two part-timers will be in so you will have help."

"Okay, everything will be fine."

"Your girl come back yes?"

"Yes, she came back last night and is getting her hair done this morning."

"You will be making romantic plans for tonight, No?"

"May see a movie but a nice dinner and drinks maybe at her favorite place."

"Gewt, gewt. Okay, I'm gone. Take care. If you need me, call me on my cell okay?"

"Okay have fun and tell everyone I said hello.

"Will do" she said and she left.

As he was logging in on the computer, Sharon from the kiosk across the hall came into the store. She was 5'5,

120lbs, a large breasted mulatto with long brown hair that fell to the center of her back. She was the first friend he made when he came to Texas and they had hung out quite a few times. She introduced him to people and was more like a sister. He was very fond of Sharon and held her in very high regard.

"Hey, you want to hang out with me, G, and Dashyn tonight? We going to go to City Lights."

"I would but Camille got back and we are going to go out for a bit. Catch up you know?"

"Camille! she said questionably "Oh how is she?"

"She is good just glad to be back."

"Oh, okay so if y'all don't mind, just come on through. It will be fun you know how we do."

"Yeah you know I will because I could use a good night out."

"Yeah, Shania would want to see you too as well."

"Yeah I bet she would like to see the hell out of me"

They both started laughing.

"Okay just think about it and let me know okay?"

"Okay."

The store was slow and the part-timers showed up. It was around 1 p.m. when the call came through.

"Thank you for calling Athlete's Foot this is Robert how may I help you?"

"Yes, I'm looking for Robert is he in?" The man's voice said.

"Yes, this is Robert how may I help you?"

"You're the person I've been waiting to talk to you. Do you have a minute as we really need to discuss something in person? Can you meet me at 3 p.m. at The Barracks?"

"Who is this?" he asked.

"This is Brandon," the man said.

Robert's heart sank into his stomach a bit but was curious to talk to this Brandon.

"This must be the same Brandon from the letters."

"Yes, one and the same, and I think we should really talk in person. Can you come to The Barracks at 3 p.m. today?"

"What is this about," he said knowingly.

"I'd rather tell you in person. I think it's some things we should discuss. Some things aren't right."

"Okay, where will you be in The Barracks?"

"I'll meet you where you normally park off Tank Battalion. I'll be standing outside waiting."

"Okay, I'll see you at 3."

Robert hung up the phone. Janet walked in during the conversation, so he knew he would be able to make the meeting with Brandon. He always had his suspicions now he would be able to obtain clarity. He drove home, grabbed his snub nose .38 revolver and his leather gloves. Being new in the area not knowing what could happen, he knew to always take precaution.

He tucked the .38 in the small of his back and headed for the base. He stopped at McDonald's off Rancier Ave to stash the gun so the guards on the base could not find it when he went through the clearance. Once on base, he stopped in the parking lot of Darnell Hospital and placed the gun back into his lower back. When he pulled into the barracks he saw a man about his age, slightly taller standing with three other guys. He pulled his .38 from his back and stuck it in the front of his belt. He got out of the car and approached the men.

"Hey, do y'all know a guy named Brandon?"

"I'm Brandon," the guy in the middle said extending his hand.

Robert shook it. Not beating around the bush Brandon got straight to the point. He confirmed Robert's thoughts as to who he was and in fact, was very much involved with Camille. He said he approached her about him when he came in the limo, he said no guy who thought it was over would do anything like that and wanted to say something then but she kept saying that Robert wouldn't let her go. He bought the other three guys as witnesses to her actions because she had also been involved with them. Robert's heart was in his stomach. He was hurt, and he was hurt bad. He couldn't understand how he was still standing after hearing this devastating news.

Here he was, standing in front of the guys who had been sleeping with his fiancé. He wanted to burst into tears and explode. The world was spinning in a massive vortex of emotional pain riddled with humiliation, ridicule, and deceit. He wanted to run but his legs were too heavy. Like a deer in headlights of a speeding truck, he couldn't move in time, hearing the roar prior to the massive collision that would ultimately take his life. He wanted to kill them all right where they stood. He had his gun but the pain he felt was worse than any bullet could inflict. He thought this must be what death feels like. Little was he aware of how close he was about to get that night.

JULY 2004 JILLIAN'S

―――――

"Would you all like to start with something to drink or do you need a moment?" the young brunette waitress said.

"We can do both" Camille said.

Jasmin placed her order of salmon with salad. When Robert was about to speak, Camille cut him off.

"I will have the hot wings with the steak medium well and the gentleman will have the same" Robert looked at her incredulously. "But make the steak well done" and she smiled at him.

'She remembered' he thought. The waitress took the order and before she walked off he said looking at her "Extra blue cheese for the wings." She nodded in saying 'You remember'.

Jasmin sat back looking at the two of her friends and what seemed like a glimpse of hope. He cut the moment short going back to his original position.

"Things are so different now Camille, so am I, and I don't see how we would work out. I moved on, and after what I found out then so have you."

"I made a mistake but I would hardly call it moved on. Brandon wasn't right for me, you were. It took me losing you to see that. Now all I want is my man back."

"Your man back?"

"Yes, my man back Robert. I know what happened was bad but what we had was strong and I know you just don't forget that level of love. I know that seems crazy coming from me" she held out her palms. "But it is the truth. I still love you and deep down I can see it in your eyes you still love me."

She touched his right hand. His phone rang. It was his friend from Philly. Another memory resurfaced about her at the wrong time. He sent the call to voicemail.

"I need to use the ladies' room," Jasmin said.

"So do I" Camille joined before she asked him to order them more drinks.

'Already telling me what to do' he thought.

He ordered more drinks and waited on them to return. They returned refreshed. Their drinks and food had arrived. They talked more about his music and her being in nursing. She was always ambitious so it was no surprise and all for nothing he always had a thing for nurses. They talked more and managed to even laugh a little. Dinner was over and Camille was about to pay the bill but he stopped her. He paid the bill and left the waitress a really nice tip.

They were all back to their cars and they waved bye to Jasmin. They sat and talk a little longer, exchanged numbers, and with a kiss on the cheek bid each other goodnight. He opened her door and told her he would call her. Three days later they met at his apartment complex and just talked for a while. Camille told him more about Brandon and her leaving the military. She told him Brandon was in North Carolina with her and had a job. It was then he knew what he would do.

FORT HOOD 2001

"Where is she now?" Robert asked.

"She is in the Barrack unloading clothes."

"She told me she was going to get her hair done."

"Nah man she been unpacking, and I called when I saw the Iceberg shirt 'cause I asked her where she got it from. She told me it was her brothers."

"No, it's mine."

"I figured."

Brandon and Robert devised a plan to surprise her while she was unpacking. Brandon would walk in first then leave the door open and Robert would come in seconds later since she wouldn't see him walk in. When Brandon walked in she saw him walking up the hall while she unpacked clothes.

"Hey babe," she said to him.

"Hey" he responded.

Robert was standing at the door. He then walked in to see his fiancé unpacking clothes. She looked like a deer in headlights.

"Hey babe," he said sarcastically. She was speechless. "Oh, you didn't know I knew Brandon huh?" She was motionless and emotionally shocked. "Give me my ring you lying bitch."

"It's upstairs, and I'm not a bitch."

"Yes you are, and I want my ring back."

"You told me that you and him were done. You lied to me and him" Brandon said.

"My Ring! Now!"

She just reached on the dresser, grabbed her purse, and pulled out the ring that sat in a small compartment. "Wow! You ain't shit. Who is it going to be me or him?" Robert asked.

He thought maybe she would say him but when she said Brandon he couldn't get away fast enough. He didn't want either one of them to see his tears. He got back into his car and drove back to Harker Heights but stopped by The Liquor Barn and bought a bottle of Remy Martin black.

When he got to his apartment, he couldn't hold it anymore. He collapsed right in the doorway and cried harder than he had ever cried in his life.

He finally pulled himself up off the floor and grabbed the bottle. He began to drink. He drank hard and heavy and the more he drank the more it hurt. The more it hurt, the more he drank. The thought came to end it all and the more he drank the better it seemed. How could she have done this to him? He came all the way to Texas for her. He left his family for her. He changed his life for her. He would have done anything for her. He looked at his gun. He drank some more until he got the nerve. He drank the rest and went to the medicine cabinet and grabbed some pills. He was going to take all the pain away.

HARKER HEIGHTS 2001

"9-1-1 emergency how may I help you?"

"Jes, I need an ambulance to two oh one Lookout Ridge Apartments."

"What is the problem, ma'am?"

"I'm thinking my employee just try kill himself."

"Where is he, ma'am?"

"He is lying on floor with foam in mouth."

"Is he breathing?"

"Is barely breathing, the pulse is light please come quickly."

"Is he bleeding ma'am?"

"No, I think he took pills please hurry."

"Help is on the way ma'am please stay on the phone."

"Yes! Yes! please hurry!"

2004 CONCORD NORTH CAROLINA

———————

Brandon sat in the passenger seat while Camille picked him up from working 3rd Shift at the distribution center. Camille looked as if she was up all night long. When he asked was she okay she told him that she was. He knew she was lying but it didn't matter as he was already prepared to go back to New York. Just like years back when he made a call, he had received a call from a familiar voice. The same voice who met him at work just nights before telling him what was about to happen. He knew that Robert deserved this moment, especially after he almost took his own life over Camille.

Robert told him all about Camille's dinner and what he intended to do. He would fuck her one last time and make her feel they would be together, but the truth was that they wouldn't nor should Brandon stay. Brandon agreed and made plans to leave Camille shortly after but would allow certain guys to break into her place and take all of their items. He would leave that very day after their daughter was dropped at the sitter. "We need to talk," Camille said to Brandon. He just looked at her.

REASON 4

HE'S AN ILLEGANIST

The Illeganist is similar to the Mandingo as they both are maturations of history, so even though responsible for their own acts, you must account for his history. This way, you can properly negate if you can value his reason. One point I will make, which is the Illeganist's biological reason for cheating, is not only his fault, but it's the partners as well. Have you ever heard of polygamy? It's been around for centuries and it's a known practice with Muslims and monarchs. Tribal Africans would have multiple wives but only at the wife's direst to help with the work for the house. The husband could not just go all willy-nilly, taking women as wives as he pleased.

However, some monarchs of villages could do so for whatever reason. I believe currently the King of Swaziland has about 15 wives. One main, and the rest called "sister-wives", still keeping a similar approach of agreeing to bring someone in to help out with the family... Not just because the husband thinks she is hot. He also must be financially stable to conceive such an addition, yet just like a polygamist, an Illeganist operates similarly.

The Illeganist will cheat but you will probably know about it. What?! You ask? Yeah! Check this out. Have you ever known someone to date a guy who you knew slept with other women? It was accepted just as long as it did not complicate their personal interest. Cougars are pretty understanding of the Illeganist or better, women over 40 years old. They have kids or have been married and typically just don't need the headache of a relationship. They even provide financial support to the Illeganist and he normally doesn't hold a job.

If he does have a kid, the kid is considered an illegitimate as he only comes by once a week. That is normally to have sex and keep the woman off guard. The woman who is involved can only visit him by request. If he is in a household with kids that are not his he probably only takes on the role of a disciplinarian. Friends of the women who are involved with an Illeganist, are probably involved with one themselves, but are quick to tell the woman she is stupid for dealing with him. You know someone like that don't you girl?

He just goes from woman to woman as if he has no care in the world. He borrows your car, money, eats all your food, and is somewhat of a... well a parasite.

ALL women of different wealth classes go through this so it is not just poor or rich. So why is this acceptable? Beats the hell out of me, but it is and since it is, you may as well know about it. The Illeganist is big in today's millennium and they are normally young, between 18 and 35+ish, but they are getting older by the day. If you happen to meet an Illeganist, he will most likely be the most nonchalant type that you could ever meet. You would find yourself chasing him to commit versus his pursuing you in the form. Remember the Illeganist cheats because the women he cheats with know and does not care.

So be mindful of you losing yourself over someone who basically considers cheating a lifestyle. How does the old saying go? "No sense in keeping the whole pig when you just want the sausage." Well hell, you've got to watch the sausage for that matter. Don't be that person that looks in the mirror and says, "Self! Why did I put me in this ridiculous predicament?" Because self is going to say, "Cause you're stupid!"

SOLE SIREN

ASTORIA, NEW YORK

***

"Maybe I can ask my boss for a raise. He is an understanding guy you know? Plus, he does a lot of philanthropy work in the community. I'm sure if I explain the situation he would give me a loan. I would just pay it off by working more overtime."

"Don't be silly Sheila. You have done enough already for us and working overtime or even a second job may max you out...don't need you getting sicker than you are."

"I won't get sicker than I am Dan. I haven't had an attack in I don't know how long. It's been years."

"Yes, I know Sheila, but Sickle Cell Anemia is nothing you should exhaust. Last time we were rushing you to the hospital, I thought I almost lost you."

"You didn't lose me, though did you?" She wrapped her arms around his waist placing her head on his chest. "Plus, I don't think God would want me to go just yet because you would burn down the house trying to boil water" she laughed.

"Hey I can boil water I resent that. I may not know how to cook what goes in the water, but I can certainly boil it."

"Ha!" she shouted.

"I don't think God would want you to go either as He knows I wouldn't last a day alone with your kids".

She punched him in the ribs. "Hey, don't talk about my kids. They will be yours one day you know? You take me, you take them. That's the deal."

"Yeah! Yeah! I know. Sometimes I think they hate me though."

"No way! They love you, hell you're the closest example they have ever had to a father. Brady praises you all the time about you showing him things in football and Kayla just acts tough. She really does love you."

"It's only because I buy her stuff that's all."

"Oh, is that right?"

"Yes."

"And what about me?"

"What about you?"

"I don't know. Sickle Cell must have got your brain all worn out lady" he kissed her.

102

"Well, I can think of something else that could wear me out."

"Oh yeah?" he asked.

"Yeah," she said looking him in the eyes. They kissed passionately as they lay on the bed. Dan started to unbutton her blouse when a knock came to the door.

"Mom!"

"Yes!"

"Can I come in?"

"What is it, Kayla?"

"Can I come in?" Dan rolled over and Sheila buttoned her blouse. Kayla came in with Taylor, her friend from school.

"Can you take me and Taylor to Britney's house?"

"In a minute Kayla, and how long are you staying because I have to go to the office."

"Just for a while. I was going to spend the night at her house."

"Okay. Just let me get situated."

"Okay," Kayla said.

"Hi, Dan," Taylor said.

"Hi, Taylor" he responded.

Dan was fond of Taylor and called her his second daughter because she was always at their house. He looked after her just like he did Kayla. He even bought her Christmas and birthday presents. The girls left, and Sheila asked for a rain check. He went to the closet to change shirts. Sheila eyed his 6'8 frame that used to play professional football before his knee injury. He like many other athletes from the pros, got into doing private security detail, as it was a thriving industry that allowed him to mingle with some of the elite. He got his job after a fellow teammate informed him of the opportunity when his client made specific requirements of his personal security.

Now, Dan McCallihan aka Ireland was a pillar of Mr. Louis's security team, one he took extremely seriously. Dan got dressed and took out a cell phone to send out a text to Domingo to work out, but he had a message from Mr. Louis that he wanted him to stop by the lounge then meet him at his office on Broadway. He figured that be good as any time to see if Mr. Louis checked his proposal about financial security options for ex-football players. Although he was an ex-football player he majored in finance and was Series 7 certified. His approach to Mr. Louis was one that did catch his attention; so much in fact that they discussed it on occasion. He thought he wouldn't rush Mr. Louis. He will let it come on its own, yet Sheila was getting ill more often and the money for the bills would be a big help.

Sheila works for Royal, Oak, and Garden the law firm, but her divorce still left her in debt. He loves Sheila and sympathized when she told him about her illness when they met years ago when Mr. Louis became a client of Royal Oak and Garden. Jenna introduced them, and they were inseparable ever since. He also knew how life was for ex-pro athletes. Most didn't have the proper insurances that cover the after-effects of the league. Some were in so much debt that they pawned or sold their championship rings. Some didn't have the money and owed a lot in gambling.

Others went to a life of drug-dealing, something Dan would never do, but his friend was another story. Speaking of his delinquent friend, where was he? He didn't show up to work out this morning like they normally did on Mondays. He made it a point to call Domingo. Sheila dropped Kayla and Taylor off at their friend's house and was heading by the office with Brady since he enjoyed going into the large skyscraper. She would only be there momentarily then she would hurry home to start a late ordering of dinner which happened more times than she would have liked, but it was how things were for the moment.

105

She was optimistic that things would get better though. She had to sign in even though she had clearance to the building. Mr. Wade, the security guard, was an elder in his 60s but years from being an Army Ranger, and boxing kept his physique and wit about him in the image of 40. He was a delight for those who were known in the building. He was also stern and took his job very seriously...until kids were involved anyway.

"Is that my main man Brady?" his 6'2 frame sat viewing over the front desk.

"Hi Wade" Sheila said

"Hi, Mr. Wade. It's me. Mr. Wade, I grew a whole inch since you last saw me."

"Did you now? Well, you keep growing at this rate, and you'll be taller than this building by tomorrow."

"What!? I can't be taller than this building Mr. Wade. Humans can't grow to be that tall."

"They can if they are Stretch Armstrong" he presented Brady with the famous rubber figure.

"Wow, Mom look! Mr. Wade got me a Stretch Armstrong. Isn't it awesome? "

"Yes. What do you say?"

"Thanks, Mr. Wade. You are the coolest" he smiled.

Looking at Sheila Mr. Wade said "I don't think I've ever been the coolest before. That's a new one."

"You don't know what you have started Wade."

"Yes, I do. You're all clear here if you need anything just give me a buzz."

"Okay I won't be long," she said. "Come on Brady." They reached the 26th floor to her office. While Brady rushed to the window with his Stretch Armstrong she sat at her desk, logged in, then opened files for her boss that she needed to send to another firm.

"Are those the McArthur files you're transferring?" Ed Royal said standing at the door.

"Yes, sir I just sent them, and I cc'd Patricia Markson as well. We should be all set for the meeting on Monday."

"Well done. I swear if we didn't have your diligence this firm would not stand as sturdy as it does."

"Thank you, Mr. Royal," she said. She liked working for the firm as they were fair to all of their employees. On occasion, at the firm, you may catch them in a boy's club chuckle, but at the Christmas parties and retreats they were the funniest old men you would ever meet. Especially Ed Royal. He was always showing up with some young model type that could be his youngest daughter.

"Hi, Mr. Royal."

"Well my goodness Brady I almost didn't recognize you. My how you've grown."

Mom makes me eat brussels sprouts but I don't like them."

"You don't say?"

"Yes, I do say, but she makes me eat them anyway."

"They're good for you," Sheila said.

"Then why do they taste so yucky?" Brady asked.

She looked at Mr. Royal who shrugged.

"Kids got a point. See you on Monday Sheila after my much-needed week off and you take care young Brady."

"Bye Mr. Royal" Brady waved his Stretch Armstrong.

He waved and was gone.

"One more thing and we are out of here okay?"

"Okay," he said, turning back to the window looking at the view.

She sent an email to the finance department.

CONDE NAST

D an stopped by the lounge to grab some documents. Now, he was at Mr. Louis's office off of Broadway. Although he loved the club he really enjoyed going to the main office with all the tourists buzzing around the famous attraction. Even as a kid from Medina New York his father would bring him and his sister Teresa to see the ball drop and watch The Macy's Thanksgiving Day Parade. He also didn't mind seeing all the models that went to the Teen Vogue and GQ Magazine floors.

A lot of them would be visiting or handling business and he never knew who he would meet that would make Kayla just ooze in awe. He saw Carolina Panthers quarterback Cam Newton fall off his Segway in the street in Uptown Charlotte while on a trip with Mr. Louis. He didn't have his phone out in time but when he told Brady he just couldn't stop laughing. When Dan got off the elevator Holly Emil, Mr. Louis's secretary was on the phone and waved him towards Mr. Louis's office door. He waved hello to her and she did the same.

"Knock! Knock! It's me boss" sticking his head into the large oak door.

"Come in Dan, come in."

"Here are the papers you requested from the lounge, and I doubled with Franco to make sure the changes to the glasses were to be made before opening tonight."

"How did he take it?"

"He had a fit just like you said he would."

"Ha! I knew it" motioning for Dan to have a seat. Dan set the black binder down on the large black desk.

"Man, this view is incredible. I can never get over it."

"Yeah, I remind myself of that every time I sit in this chair. Always told myself that never giving up got me to where I wanted to be in life."

"I hear that boss."

"I went from $0.30 noodles showing my papers on federal yards to eating steaks with views of skyscrapers... Spent a lot of time dreaming."

"Oh, I know the feeling sir!

"I know Dan. I can see it in you as well big guy. Keep striving and it will come to you, you know?"

"Yes sir, I will keep that in mind. So, what's new boss? I know tonight is my night off, but can I help with anything?"

"Well, Dan that's why I wanted to see you. See I have a ..."

The phone rang.

"Excuse me" Mr. Louis pressed the intercom on his phone. "Yes, Holly?"

"Miss Rodriguez is here to see you, sir."

"Please send her in. Thank you" he pushed the button to 'off'.

As he looked up, Korina Rodriguez walked into the office. She wore her hair in a tight ponytail, wearing red square-framed clear lens glasses, a black fitted long sleeve v-neck shirt that exposed her bust, fitted black skinny jeans, and red bottom heels. Although casual she still wore a professional aura. She was gorgeous, as it seemed she glided as she walked through the room. Robert walked around the desk to greet her.

"How are you, my dear? You look amazing" taking her hand and kissing her cheek.

"I am well, thank you, darling. Sorry, it took me so long to get away. The shoot took longer than expected. I also ran into GQ and ran into Morgan. You know how we two get chatty."

"Yes, I do. How is Mojo anyway?"

"She is well. She told me to tell you she is still on the logistics of what you two discussed but will get with you later to go over all the details."

"Hmmm Okay. Honey, you remember Dan from my security detail?" Dan nodded.

"Ms. Rodriguez, pleased to see you again."

"Yes, Ireland of course. How are you?"

"I'm well thank you for asking, and yourself?"

"I'm tired but out here trying to make a name for myself you know?"

"Yes, yes I do. I've seen your work and you seem to be popping up everywhere now, and the movie was great."

"You saw The Queen?"

"Yeah. I was at the screening."

"I had Ireland, Bishop, and Domingo up in the rise as patrons. One can never be too careful" Mr. Louis said.

"Oh, well then I'm glad you not only like the movie but was there to keep us safe."

"No problem ma'am, just doing my job" Dan looked between her and Mr. Louis.

"And what a great job you've been doing. So great in fact this moment allows me to inform you why I have both of you here" Korina and Dan looked puzzled.

"I want you to be Korina's exclusive protection detail." Dan was shocked, but Korina was cool as a fan when she gave a slight smile to Robert then Dan.

ASTORIA, NEW YORK

"He wants you to do what?"

"To be Korina's exclu..."

"Exclusive detail I heard you," Sheila said cutting him off. "What does that mean exactly?"

"It means I would be her bodyguard."

"So now this bitch thinks she's Whitney Houston."

"Mom!"

"Sorry, Brady don't use bad words."

"That's a dollar mom."

"I know Brady.

"I'm going to be rich! Woohoo! Come on Tater" he and the brown pit-bull ran to his room to get his piggy bank.

"I'm no Kevin Costner, but yes I'll be her new bodyguard."

"But why you? Why not Brooklyn, Domingo or Bishop?"

"He thought I would be a better fit, I don't know."

"Yet you didn't refute it either did you?"

"No, because it meant more money and babe we could use it."

"I know, and I'm happy for you, and I'm grateful you were thinking of us, but she is just so...ughhh!...and the whole thing with Kim's part in the movie...nobody has heard from her in weeks it seems. Now you have to be around her. I just don't like it."

Yeah, I'm not a total fan of it either yet as I said it does bring us extra money and if this goes well who knows maybe Mr. Louis will give me the seed capital for GCB."

"Hey speaking of GCB..."

"Mom where's my bank?" Brady shouted.

"It should be on your dresser."

"I know but it's not there."

"Did you move it?"

"No! Mom it's always there I never move it" he came back downstairs with Tater following. He sat at the table with worry on his face.

"I'll help you look for it bud, okay?" Dan said.

"OK," Brady said looking sad.

"How much you think you got anyway?" Dan asked.

"$300 almost," Brady said courageously.

115

"Oh wow! You must have been saving for a long time" Dan said.

"No! You all just curse a lot."

"Well, we'll have to tone it down then."

"No way I need you to keep it up so I can get the new Y2F250 bike so I can work on my Supercross moves."

"Wow really?"

"Yes. I'll be a Las Vegas Supercross winner one day."

"Well we'll be right there to root you on," Dan said.

"I wonder where it could be," Sheila said.

They had dinner, watched a movie, and went to bed.

BROOKLYN NEW YORK

INDIGO HOTEL 11 a.m. (Monday)

The Asian room attendant didn't get a response when knocking on Kim's door.

"Room service!" she called again.

She used her key to open the door backing her cart in and closing the door. She turned and almost fell over startled at the mess of the room. She looked at the bed noticing clothes, so she knew the occupant was still staying in the room. She would just need to be quick about it. She moved the clothes that were on the bed to the table that mounted the TV. She stripped the bed linens, balling them up and placing them in a hamper on her cart. She reached on the second shelf of her cart grabbing new linens and a pillowcase.

She quickly remade the bed with two sheets, a blanket, and covered four pillows with new pillowcases. She picked up trash that was around the bed and wiped the powder off the nightstand. People are so messy she thought. She returned to her cart to grab the towels for the bathroom. She started to open the door then realize she had to get some soap for the bathroom. She grabbed two soap bars and headed toward the bathroom. She turned the knob on the door, but the door didn't open. She pushed again but it did not open.

"Hello! Room service!" she called. "Do you need cleaning?"

No answer. She tried the door again, but it didn't give way. Something is blocking the door she thought. She considered calling maintenance but gave the door one last push with the bump of her hip. The door flew open and what she saw made her jump back into the room. She fell against the cart. She reached as quickly as she could for her walkie-talkie. She called the front desk and frantically told the desk clerk to call 911. The woman in the room she was cleaning was dead...

Yo bro where are you? -Ireland

(no reply) -Domingo

Got a new gig bro, call me when

you get this -Ireland.

HOLLYWOOD CALIFORNIA

"**D**on't forget to check out Korina Rodriguez in the new blockbuster hit 'The Queen' in theaters now. I'm your host Vince Falcon. Until the next time Hollywood after Dark... Good night."

The crowd applauded as Korina talked more with the host as the credits rolled and shots of the audience were seen on the screen. They both stood, walked towards the crowd, and started to shake the member's hands.

'Clear!' the young PA said.

"We'll see you Korina. Tell Robert I said hello" Vince said before he walked away with an army full of people.

She too had a nice entourage. She headed back to her dressing room with her assistant, hairdresser, makeup artist, and security guard. They all praised her for a job well done and was preparing to go back to the hotel from the studio. Korina, her assistant, and Ireland were in the same vehicle as the makeup artist and hairdresser stayed behind for a second.

"We need to make an appearance at Pure while we are here as it will look good for you," her assistant said. "We don't need to stay the whole time but it would be good to not only get that support but also show you are supporting Robert's Pure Lounge west coast."

"Okay that sounds like a plan but I want to get into something more comfortable ok?"

"We can go by the hotel ... Dan!" Melissa said.

"Don't bother" Korina said as she reaches for her bag in the back. "I have something I can slip on. To Pure Ireland. Take your time" Korina said while she was just over his shoulder.

"Yes Korina," he said looking over his shoulder noticing her hand around his bicep.

She sat back and began to kick off her heels. Malissa was on the phone confirming their arrival to Pure. Dan was watching the road but couldn't help to notice Korina eyeing him from the backseat. Korina saw Malissa was into her phone and iPad then took the chopsticks out of her hair. It fell over her shoulders in thick wavy locks. She ran her fingers through it slowly. She then unbuttoned her blouse down the center exposing her size D breasts in a black lace bra. Dan was looking at her as if he was in a trance. She reached her right arm behind her back and with the flick of her fingers her bra detached. She used both hands to remove it from the straps leaving her breasts exposed. She rubbed them slowly looking back from her breast to Dan in the mirror.

Dan kept switching his view between the road and Korina. He caught Malissa looking at him then he quickly looked back to the road. Malissa exchanged quick glances with Korina, then back to Dan, who was now fully fixated on the road. Malissa sat her phone and iPad down as Korina looked at her while taking off her skirt revealing her black lace panties. Malissa saw this and removed her black-rimmed glasses as Korina slid down her panties, hitting the recline button on the side of the chair.

Dan took another glimpse in the rearview mirror. He could feel the blood rush below his waist. Malissa had removed her black sweater revealing her plump C cup breast in red lace. She lowered her right and left strap and unclasped her bra from the front. Korina was reclined back looking at Dan in the mirror. Malissa got out of her seat and kneeled in front of Korina. Dan's eyes darted back and forth from the road as he saw Malissa's head between Korina's legs as Korina played with her own breasts.

ASTORIA NEW YORK

"So where is Dan tonight?" Pam said to her longtime neighbor of 12 Years.

"They're in California shooting the Hollywood After Dark show."

"Oh, I love Vince Falcon he is so funny," Pam said.

"Yeah, I know. It would have been good if I could have gone, but I have to work, and the kids are here you know?"

"Yeah, I remember when Chris would take trips to Miami for the hotel. I used to love it when I could attend some trips with him. We would use them as vacation times."

"Really?"

"Oh yes dear, it was great."

"He never got upset about you wanting to be there?"

"Probably, but after I caught him with Roslyn he did everything to make sure I never thought he cheated again."

"Oh my! That had to drive him crazy."

"If anything, it drove me crazy."

"Why do you say that?"

"Because hell, I was cheating on him and I had my lover follow when we took trips, so while he worked so did my lover."

"Oh my God Pam that is so bad. How could you?"

"Pretty easy actually because my lover could always get away, so it worked out."

"You should be ashamed."

"I was and I made sure my lover punished me for it too."

"Wow!"

"Look I know it sounds bad."

"Sounds bad?"

"Well it was bad, but it was the best thing for my marriage."

Sheila listened to her friend Pam discuss her infidelity and couldn't help but wonder if Dan could ever do something like that to her. She put it out of her mind as quick as she could but the initial thought had already made a home in her head and emotions.

PURE LOUNGE

HOLLYWOOD CALIFORNIA

As Dan watched Korina, Malissa, and other celebs party, he stood in the background with the rest of the security details. He couldn't believe what he witnessed during the ride over. This kind of thing happens in movies to major stars, not to guys like him in reality. They were looking directly at him for sure. No two ways about it. She wanted him to watch. Maybe it was a test by Mr. Louis even though he would never peg Mr. Louis as a type who would try to bait him. No Mr. Louis was on the straight and narrow this was all Korina. She had always found ways to touch him or get him to see her naked.

Making comments about how large his manhood was and how she could make sure he got all that he wanted. Although it was inviting he couldn't do that to Sheila. He loved her and wanted to make sure he was nothing like the ex's she had been with because he was different. No Korina would just have to get over herself. He will be back home in a couple of days and will tell Mr. Louis he would need to switch detail and focus on GCB.

ASTORIA NEW YORK

"Have you seen your brother's
piggy bank Kayla?" -Mom

"No Mom I haven't" -Kayla.

"OK. How's everything?" -Mom

"Fine. We are just hanging out.

May go to Emily Pratt later"

-Kayla

"Okay well be careful and call me

when you get in" -Mom

"Okay, love you mommy" -Kayla.

"Love you too Kayla" -Mom

TAYLOR'S HOUSE

"Who was that?"

"It was my mom asking me about my brother's piggy bank."

"I thought you said they never mess with it."

"He doesn't but apparently my mom or Dan cursed so he was going to put money in it!"

"OMG that's so weird."

"Yeah, so I have to put the money back. Are you sure this is going to work?"

"Yes, I'm sure. You know Kaitlyn Moore?"

"Yes, everyone knows Kaitlyn."

"Well, I heard this is how she paid for her surgery and all those clothes she has."

"I thought her parents gave her all that money."

"No way babes, pops split and left her moms and her for a whole new family on the coast."

"Wow!"

"Mom drank so much they almost lost their house, so Kaitlyn did this."

"Does her mom know?"

"Hell no! And if she did, she is probably too boozed out to know what's going on. Kaitlyn tells her she gets it from her dad."

"So how are we going to keep this from getting out?"

"We will just say we got some scholarships. No one will know. So, you down?"

"I don't know Taylor what if we meet someone we know?"

"All the better because they most likely will not want anyone to know where we saw them."

"I guess you're right."

"Of course, I'm right, and once we are started you can have your brother's money back and then some, then we can go down to Miami for college together as we planned."

"Okay let's do it." They pulled out the $300 gift card they bought from the corner bodega, logged on to a website, and created a profile.

PURE LOUNGE NEW YORK

———————

Dan attempted to discuss his wanting to leave but Robert Louis asked him about GCB, and it threw him completely off. To make matters worse Korina was present and since she knew that was a way to get Dan she used it to her advantage. As long as Dan could keep her happy she would ensure that Dan would get the seed capital for his business venture. Dan had come to the conclusion that he was too close to being able to secure the funds so it wouldn't hurt. He had been with Korina on three different occasions so far and it was quite easy.

The extra money made it easy for him to keep Sheila happy with nice gifts for distractions. He came home one night smelling of perfume, but he told Sheila that he had kept Korina from a mob of fans outside the store so that was why. It made sense and the job called for close contact so she ultimately went with it. That was all he needed to do with Sheila but Mr. Louis was a different story. Things in the detail had taken a turn now that detectives came looking for Domingo, and cameras were around double what they normally would be.

Korina was catching a bit of an attitude with Mr. Louis now that she was gaining a little fame as he called it, and Dan knew that if she kept it up she would not only get blackballed but may expose her infidelity. He would have to seduce her to get Mr. Louis to fund GCB. He came up with the plan to do just that knowing Korina wouldn't be able to resist. He had to make a call he hoped he wouldn't have to make another day in his life, but it was the only way.

ASTORIA QUEENS

Sheila sat at the table by herself just staring at the envelope in front of her. She told herself it was the right thing to do, and it would make life better for her family. She believed in her relationship with Dan and knew he loved her very much. She put all the nonsense of him cheating out of her mind and for a moment, her attention shifted to the news about how Korina was getting all sorts of attention from fans. Even Kayla and Brady now talk about how their mom's boyfriend was always on the news because he worked with the famous Korina Rodriguez.

In school, it somewhat made them popular making them new friends and company at the house. More kids wanted to come over hoping they might get to see Korina, but also take selfies as one had captioned "Same security as Korina." It was all innocent, but it was kind of overbearing. She just wanted her family on one accord and focused on the future. She figured this would get Dan out of that limelight, and back to a more structured day like hers was. Yes, this was the way to go she figured holding the envelope. This would change their lives forever. She thought she would surprise him with a nice dinner at a nice place, and a weekend resort getaway for two. It will be romantic, and a memory they would share for a lifetime. As she smiled to herself she thought how much she loved Dan.

BEDMINSTER NEW JERSEY

"**H**ey you what's up?" -Ireland

"Not much, just living taking care of my

business and staying away from people

who be on some bullshit. Definitely

didn't expect to hear from you." -DW

"Yeah, I know I've been trying

to stay out of the way and get

some things done plus I knew

you were working things out

with your kids so I knew to

give you some space" -Ireland

"I and mine are straight like I

said, but feed me no bullshit.

What do you want" -DW

"I don't want shit. I'm just checking

in on you because you were on my

mind. I think of you often I just don't

132

reach out because I know you
are busy" -Ireland

"And?" -DW

"I'm still in a battle with all of this"
-Ireland

"All of this what? You mean you
actually, have feelings for me but
you with that bitch? Fuck out of
here." -DW

"Come on now I'm saying I never
thought it would be like that
between you and me. You just
hit me with all of your hidden
emotions, and I didn't know how
to handle it. We were friends and
then you say you love me. It threw
me into left field." -Ireland

"So you telling me loving you
was some bullshit right?" -DW

133

"No, it wasn't bullshit but I can't
say that I wasn't confused about
it all." -Ireland

"I knew with all the shit you
have going on I'm sure you
need to sit back and
look at what I've been trying
to tell you. That's why I remained
in my own lane and
watched from a far". -DW

"And that's just it, I think I wanted
to be in denial. I wanted to not
adhere to the I told you so but
you were right" -Ireland

"But..." -DW

"...But at the end of it all, I'm always
wondering had I known for all
those times we were around each
other, would things be different? -Ireland

"You all over the place with this
conversation and I told you that
you need to be straight with me
if you are going to talk to me" -DW

"Not what I'm saying more like
what I'm wondering" -Ireland

"Which is?" -DW

"Do you still love me?" -Ireland

"You know I love you yo. I just
love you from a distance
because I know you have all
that shit going on. I mean
with us, we are what we are
in my mind. I'm not mad or
anything I'm just doing me. You
know how I feel about you. You
know what my past is about so
why are you acting brand-new?" -DW

"Okay... So do I" -Ireland

135

Why Do Men Cheat

"So do you what?" -DW

"Love you" -Ireland

"Now this means what exactly?" -DW

"How long will it take you

to meet me where we had

drinks the last time I was in New York?" -Ireland

"20 minutes" -DW

"See you then" -Ireland

BROOKLYN BREWERY UPTOWN

Dan had been to this part of Brooklyn in the past, so he was familiar with the locals. He arrived somewhat early and took the employee entrance from the hotel as it was attached to The Indigo. The Indigo still strayed with the press that is yet to conclude after the overdose of Kim in her room. They are mainly there to keep track of the ongoing investigation, as the authorities were still on the hunt for Domingo, who was reportedly seen coming out of the hotel room by an anonymous eyewitness.

Dan knew Domingo dealt in narcotics to help him get extra money, but he never would've thought Domingo would be tied to the death of such a high-profile actress. He didn't want to try to contact him and he didn't want to be implicated in harboring a suspect in an ongoing investigation. However he wished he could help his longtime friend. He would just wait to see if he could get a call from him some way, or even a message so he could help.

Once inside he said hello to Vince the bartender who he actually met on his first trip out to New York City, then he took a seat in the back of the dining area. He ordered a double Patron and sat innocuously in the dim light. He was just finishing his drink when he saw Dominique West open the door. They met through a mutual friend who ended up becoming a mutual dislike. They talked over the years and even worked on a couple of business deals together. She was well known around her industries of interest which ranged from music, energy, restaurants, and corporate America.

She had an edge to her personality, this made her Dan's favorite. They were like siblings the way they act around each other, but one day Dominique confessed her feelings for Dan. It took him off guard and he receded in their communication. He didn't realize deep inside he stored feelings for her as well. He chalked it to the concept of a man and a woman who spend so much time talking, tend to develop some form of intimate feelings for each other.

Yet not crossing that line was the best bet in their relationship to remain friends. Dominique knew Dan loved Sheila and Dan knew he didn't want to hurt Sheila. He loved her and was very much committed to being with her. Dominique told him if he wasn't with Sheila she knew that he would be with her. Based on the way they communicated Dan knew this was very true. This very information he knew would secure his intention for the evening.

One thing he knew about Dominique and most women was that when women have an emotional attachment to you, you can virtually get them to do anything you want them to do for you. At 35 Dominique had the body of a 21-year-old. Her 5'5 120lbs frame was extremely imposing in the eyes of those who are notably recognized for being beautiful. She had large olive hazel eyes, full lips, and a gap in her teeth that looked fit for her being the perfect aphrodisiac. She would always joke to him about how immaculate her fellatio skills were.

He often, after she revealed her feelings, wondered how true that was. She was a light-skinned bombshell, but she also had an explosive temper...a big one. He stood as she was shown by the hostess where he was waiting for her. Wearing a black pea coat, jeans, shin boots, and grey scarf. Her hair was long but he noticed she cut it substantially. He gave her a warm embrace. Her small frame fitting into him like a glove. He thought the moment felt good to him.

"Mmmmm, you smell good," she said inhaling deep into his neck. It immediately sent blood rushing below his waist. He tried to laugh off the sensation.

"What's wrong with you?" she said retracting just in front of his face.

"Nothing, just a memory I had that's all."

"What memory?"

"When you told me the cologne I had on at the beach stunk". She leaned her head back at the thought.

"It didn't stink I just told you I didn't like it."

"You said it stunk."

"You're right it did stink." They both laughed for a moment still embracing each other.

"Hey, you," he said still holding her close. She squeezed him placing her palm on the back of his head pushing him closer into her.

"Hey, you" she responded softly.

"What are you drinking?" he asked as they released, pulling her chair out for her.

"I'll have what you're having, what are you having anyway? Your usual?"

"You know it."

"Okay then, in that case, make it a double."

"It's already double."

"Then double my double, and then tell me what it is I'm doing here because if it was my guess we would turn into guests," she said with her arms crossed leaning back into the chair eyeing Dan attentively.

He ordered her two double shots of Patron poured into one glass with salt and lime. When the Cuban waitress brought the drinks back Dominique whispered something in her ear. The waitress looked up at then looked back at Dominique, nodded, and walked away.

"What was that all about?"

"Depends on what you tell me, now tell me what it is that you want."

She took a large gulp of the tequila. Seeing she was attentive Dan felt he should get straight to it.

"I need your help."

"That's obvious. What's in it for me?"

"You don't even know what I need help with. Here you are discussing reward?"

"Don't need to. I know you, and you will make sure it's worth my while."

"How can you say that?"

"Because I just did. Now can you stop playing games and tell me what it is you want?" she said, leaning into the table with her elbows, drink in her right hand, swirling it in a circle with her wrist bent.

"I need your help raising some capital for a business venture I have come up with called GCB."

"Okay."

"Okay, what?"

"Okay," she said.

"Okay, you'll do it, or okay elaborate?"

"The second one," she said, looking at the salt swirl as she twirled the tequila in the glass.

"Grammar lesson or general overview?"

"The first one" she replied looking at him.

"Okay. Gem Cap Biz is a financial program I created to help stabilize and raise economic stability in urban communities. I initially was going to do it for myself, but it just seems to have a larger purpose than myself. I was at the bookstore in North Carolina when I came across this book by Jesse Powell and Hill Harper called 'The Blackman's Handbook - The Blueprint'. It was a book of essays by some prominent figures in the African American community.

There was one where it discussed how this one guy asked a former gang member why the youth gang banged. He said the ex-gang member said because we all have no life skills to survive in our Darwinistic environments. Something about that statement stood out to me. Something not only about it, but why he said it. For decades' civil rights activists and alike have been trying effortlessly to find the center of urban development to progress its people."

"And you think this Gem Cap Biz will do so?"

"Yes, I do. See while I was working with Mongo he told me all about how he was going to make money using diamonds. Saying he can go over to Africa and buy them cheap then come back here and sell them for half the yield value which could quadruple what he paid for it."

"How does that work exactly?" she asked."

"Okay so to explain that, I have to explain the process of diamond buying. See when a diamond is mined it doesn't look anything like it does when you buy it. It's actually much uglier and it's called diamond rough or a rough diamond. It looks like a rock you could pick up outside on the ground. In African countries like Namibia, Zimbabwe, Angola, DR Congo, Sierra Leone, and Botswana. Millions of rough are mined. In this process, the diamonds can be worth as low as $450-$600 per carat minus KPC and government taxes.

Once the rough is properly taxed, verified, and purchased it gets shipped to the buyer's location, in our

143

case America, via Brinks. Once it arrives at Brinks we take it to the end buyer to resell for half of the yield price. Now since it is on US soil and has proper KPC, the price goes up to about $2500-$3500 per carat as rough, yet our end buyer would buy from us for more because of what it yields. The yield is the retail price. The retail price on a good one carat, D, flawless diamond could range from $5,000-$20,000 depending on who cuts, polishes, and sells it."

"So, how does that evolve lifestyles of ex-gang members Darwinistic mentalities and influence the economic stability of urban communities?" she asked.

"By compound interest," he said.

"What?"

"Compound interest," he said again.

"I'm lost, and I need a refill hold that thought." She summoned the waitress for refills and asked for a side dish of limes.

The waitress returned quickly with the order and asked if they needed a menu. They declined for the moment and she returned to the other customers who had now entered into the Brooklyn Brewery.

"Okay continue" as she squeezed lime into her tequila.

"Where was I?" he asked.

"Compound interest" she responded.

"Right!" He took a sip of his drink. "Let's say you have a single mother of 3 that works in a Burger King, that doesn't receive financial help from her kids' father. She lives in a project that is dangerous and gang-infested. What are the chances she comes out successful with her kids all college-educated?"

"Slim."

"Very slim, but what if she had a shot?"

"Maybe a chance of hope," she said taking a sip.

"Do you think she would have hope if she had invested $50 a month for two years?"

"No."

"Why?"

"Because it's only $1,200. What kind of hope is she going to have with that?"

"None actually, but she would for $200,000."

Dominique sat her drink down and looked at Ireland in his eyes.

"Either I'm drunk or your math is completely bad."

145

"No, not really. It's simple. You're familiar with compound interest, right?"

"Yes. It's when you take an amount and keep multiplying it by two or something. 50 becomes 100, 100 becomes 200, 200 becomes 400 and so on."

"Right."

"But that don't add up with $50 a month though."

"It does if you have a million people."

Dominique sat back as the information started to register. He continued.

"If 1 million people were investing $50 per month that would be..."

"50 million dollars per month," she said cutting him off.

"Correct! And using compound interest" he said.

"That would mean a shit ton of cash."

"And hope he said."

"But what backs the $50 per month?" she asked.

"The rough diamonds... we use the $50 per month as the infusing capital, purchase the rough, then turn right back around, and sell it to the end buyer for half the yield! We just simply get a campaign out to people on the lines of receiving $200,000 in two years by investing

$50 per month. Once they see they can get that amount impulsively, it would create a commitment for them to not only engage in a healthy investment strategy but..."

"Commit to less conflictive environments and a healthier lifestyle" she finished. "Wow," she said and sat silent. She pondered for a few seconds.

"So, have you created a marketing strategy yet because I know of about 1000 approaches you could use," she said.

"True but all I need is one and that is why you are here."

"Is that the only reason I'm here?" she asked reaching for her hand over to cover his.

He looked down for a moment then moved his hand back slowly.

"I need you to co-pitch this to Robert Louis to consummate a concrete interest. He is on the fence, but I need him in the yard. He just isn't the financial backing on this, he's also the key to the mass marketing strategy."

"How so?" she looked at him with slight resent as he moved his hand.

"Robert Louis' Tuvuler app has about 678 million people who use its chat service daily. More just to post on the daily feed. If we could get him to implement GCB in some form of a partnership or supporting factor the response will be inundating."

"Jesus aged Christ, it would make you look like Warren Buffett."

"Something like that but the changes it would make would be...monumental."

"Like the Smith & Wesson album," she said.

"Yeah just like the Smith & Wesson album. How is Tek and General Steele anyway?"

"They are good. Everyone's still bummed about Sean P, but outside of that all are good."

"Send them my regards please."

"Send them yourself I'm not your friend ambassador."

"DW?"

"Alright...whatever, but you need to show up. I mean you are stomping around Brooklyn you could at least say hello in person yourself."

"I will I promise."

"Whatever!" she said smugly.

"So, what do you think?"

"What do I think about what?"

"My proposal."

"You didn't propose...not to me anyway," she said rolling her eyes.

"My business proposal DW."

"Psh! she pouted.

He looked at her and knew her wheels were turning. After a moment she looked at him then leaned in closer to the table.

"Let's go upstairs and finish this conversation."

"DW come on now, this is serious."

"I know it is, and so is this", dropping her eyes down motioning to her vagina.

"I know it is beautiful, but I'm trying to focus here and you're not making it easy."

"Oh, I can make it easy for you. All you have to do is sit back and enjoy big boy."

"I can't," he said.

"Oh yes, you can. Remember, I've seen you in action. Remember the lesbian you slept with at the beach?"

"Wow!"

"Yeah, that's what I said when I saw you fucking her. That's why I came in and slapped you on the ass."

"I can't DW you know that. That was the old me."

"So, what's the new you?"

"The new me is with Sheila."

Dominique's hand hit the table hard, rattling the silverware and glasses.

"Fuck that bitch! Don't mention that bitch's name around me I told you." She was heated, and people were taking notice as the brewery filled considerably.

"Calm down please!" he pleaded.

"I am, calm you know I don't like that bitch" she fumed.

"Okay, I'm just saying I'm not trying to go down that road that's all."

"The hell you aren't," she said finishing her drink.

"What do you mean?" Dan asked.

"I mean if you want my help then you are going to fuck me and fuck me you're going to do...Now."

She got up and went to the waitress. She spoke a few words and the waitress reached under the counter and pulled out an envelope. She walked back to the table grabbing her coat, and scarf.

150

"Come on let's go" she demanded. He stood.

"Where?"

"To fuck, you dumb shit"

"Wait a second"

He was trying to gather his bearings, and follow her, leaving enough for the bill and tip. He placed $200 on the table, then he followed Dominique to the elevator through the glass doors connecting the brewery to The Indigo.

"That's what I want," she said when he caught up.

"What?" he asked again trying to buy time to think.

"You to fuck me" she pushed the 6th-floor button.

"Will you keep your voice down? Jesus!"

She turned to him as if he had to be kidding. The elevator opened, and she walked in and he followed. An elderly couple came in behind them. They nodded to Dominique and Dan with them reciprocating the same respectful gesture.

"Good evening. 4 please" the man said.

"Oh! Butch, I think I left the key in the car," the woman said nervously.

"You sure Sherry? Check your purse again."

"I did. My goodness, we have to go back down."

"Okay, we can don't get so worked up. I'll go out and have a look. You just sit tight in the lobby when we get back down okay?"

"Okay. I promise without you I lose my mind" she said.

"Well it's been 60 years of marriage I think I got a handle on it," he said looking at Dan and Dominique.

They smiled at the elder male whose wife was nervous trying to figure out where the key was. They stopped on the 4th floor. The door opened and two girls about 17/18 got on and pushed Lobby. The door closed and went to the 6th floor. The blonde girl was looking puzzled at Ireland in the reflection of the doors. She and her friend took a selfie. The doors opened to the 6th floor and Ireland and Dominique got off saying good evening to the remaining occupants of the elevator. He followed her trying to reason with her.

"Look! We can't do this. It's not right, and it's not the way to go about it DW."

She ignored him and walked on to room 635. She took the key out of the envelope and slid it in the lock until it lit up green on the keypad connecting the door lock. He grabbed the knob and she looked at him with tears in her eyes.

"Hey!" he said trying to settle her down.

She pushed the door open and walked in. She threw the key on the TV stand and began to remove her scarf, jacket, sweater, and boots.

"Wait," he said.

She just kept undressing. He stood at the door as he watched her navy-blue bra hit the floor. She looked at him with her hands on her hips.

"I can't," he said somberly.

She walked to him, took his hands and placed them around her waist. She stood on her tiptoes to kiss him on the lips. He didn't respond. She stood on her tiptoes again and kissed him again. He didn't respond. Tears filled her eyes as she tried to kiss him one more time harder and more passionately. He didn't respond. The tears were flowing down her face as she stepped back embarrassed. She stood crying holding herself arms crossed over her breasts.

"Get out," she said.

He looked at her and touched her elbow stepping in close. She turned away from him as the tears were warm running down her cheeks embarrassed and ridiculed. She felt completely humiliated. She stepped away from him.

"I'm sorry. Please understand" he said.

She turned and slapped him hard across his face breaking the silence of the room with a sharp crack.

"Get out!" she screamed with fire in her eyes.

He turned and walked out the door. He stood just outside the door with his head leaned forward on it. Dominique fell to her knees and cried on the floor holding herself.

REASON 5

HE'S A SWEET TALKER

Listen, how many times is it going to take for you to
get your heartbroken to realize that you're more than
just a pretty face or sexual object? How much of your
sanity are you willing to risk before you're so scarred, that
by the time a guy that does deserve you comes around,
you lose them because you can't trust men? How long
is it going to take for you to get tired of getting it wrong
when it comes to men? Don't you deserve better? You
deserve someone who is going to make sure your smile
never ends up in the wrong hands again. Don't you
agree? Sure you do, and that's why you would be
cheated on right now had a guy been saying that to
you.

The Sweet Talker knows how to play off words and your
emotions. He cheats because some women are
vulnerable and somewhat a bit naive. He will mostly
approach the ones who wouldn't see themselves with a
guy like him. He would then make them feel as if they
were on top of the world. Most women have fallen
victim to this guy and the truth to it is, it's because you
talk too much. Yeah, I said it. That communication box

155

of yours gets you into more trouble than you realize. You go on and on about your past relationships and why you're single that you basically give Sweet Talker the 'how-to-manipulate-you' manual.

All the while he is just waiting to see what else you're going to give him. The best way to avoid a Sweet Talker is to not give him the ammo to do it with. Your flaws are his gain, and when you mix dates, flowers, alcohol, and savior treatments you're as good as hooked. Stay out of that candy shop because it's stickier to get out of than you think...

REASON 6

HE'S A TEACHER

As crazy as this is going to sound, the teacher is the most beneficial cheater to experience. He's also the most hurtful. Just like his name "Teacher" implies, he is both academically and non-academically represented. His experience, as much as his reason, is more divine than it is of a selfish reason. He is the unexplainable, misleading, long-term test that counts but doesn't. Like the ACT compared to the SAT. Both scored well enough can get you into college, but one holds more weight.

The teacher is amazing to women like that perfect black heel, that goes well with that perfect dress, ending the evening with the perfect experience. The teacher is everything you could ever want, all balled up into one amazing guy. He's smart, funny, he listens, he's supportive, he is liked by your family and friends, he is introducible to your kids, he's a man about town, he cooks, he is domesticated, he is fun, his sex is great, he cuddles, and plays with your hair until you fall asleep...Ahhhh.

He holds your hand, he looks you in your eyes when you talk, he buys you flowers just because he is thinking about you, he takes you to lunch, he makes dinner dates, he always kisses you, is athletic, knows your likes, is romantic, and is stable. The guy even knows your cycle pain relief medication and knows what pads to buy for goodness sakes... so what's wrong with him right? How can he be a cheater if he does all this amazing stuff for and with you? He's too good to be true that's why he cheats, right? Wrong!

You have to ask yourself a basic question which is "How could a guy be so perfect with you cheat?" Well, the truth is the teacher is all of what most women want out of a man. 99% of available women will probably experience the teacher, yet 99% will not understand what happened to happily ever after with him when he cheats either. The teacher makes everything about a relationship work as the opposite sex until "The Moment" happens. Once the moment happens you're pretty much done for, and it will not be long before you say those four magical words. Now what you can't do is think that the teacher doesn't have every intent on making you a bride.

Heck in some cases Teacher even pops the question believe it or not. Deep down inside the teacher is all systems go with your heart, and even he is looking forward to the honeymoon in Fiji. But as fate will have it the teacher is going to rip out your guts, pull out your heart, drizzle them with your tears, and eat them in your face, all while drinking your sorrows with the girl he has started seeing. He is not officially started to see her, but she has been seeing him. He is starting to see why you no longer are his interest.

The teacher cheats on you because unconsciously your time is up for the length of availability of his time for you to pass as an equal. Huh? What? Yeah! He cheats because he feels you no longer serve an equal position. He looks at you as if you do not simply have what it takes to make the final commitment, jump the broom, go to the moon, the fireworks...what have you. Most of the time it's the things he says that "doesn't matter", but then turns out to matter as time progresses. He will vaguely bring this issue to your attention hoping you take heed.

The thing about this is, it will take years before it takes its major effect. Sometimes if you are lucky it will be months. He is called Teacher because he listens to all the wrong things you went through and not only tries to fix it but also shows you how he is different. He will be patient, and amazing to the eye as if he is really going to take his time with you to sort out whatever baggage from the past that you need to deal with.

159

Yet what you don't see is him hoping you learn what he needs you to, so you both can enter the happily ever after. You typically don't, and you end up telling everyone it's over. His family, as well as yours, are effected. This normally happens around the 4-6-year mark or sooner. You're probably living with each other in some cases, and you two may even have a child together. Internally that clock that approaches the thing that matters, you have not closed the door on.

Whatever has reserved you from fixing the issue is not allowing either of you to commit so at that point you no longer have time with him. Again, it will have taken him time to teach you he was the solution to such a matter, but for some reason you never allowed it to sink in, even when it was directly addressed. So instead of hearing wedding bells with all your friends and family, saying congratulations we're so proud, and you did well. You will hear your doorbell ring, your friends will come over, you will play it all back in your head of what you will not do next time, and you will say "I've learned my lesson."

LOVING MAHOGANY

It was once said that you never experienced love until you have truly felt pain...real pain. That's when love would show you how influential it could really be when it comes to relationships. Robert remembered after high school when he had met this girl named Mahogany that attended the University of North Carolina at Charlotte. She worked at the Bi-lo grocery store in Concord North Carolina just off Highway 29. This had to be around the year 2000.

Mahogany was originally from New York, but her parents moved to Winston-Salem North Carolina. She was African American and Puerto Rican, and one fine woman to him. They were both 21 years old at the time, just trying to figure out life. He worked at the store the summer before. She had flawless caramel skin, big brown eyes, and a body of an Olympic sprinter. He was instantly captivated by her natural beauty. She was...what's the word...feminine. You know, the extremely girly type. She was very polite and likable so approaching her was easy. He immediately started to put their similarities about them together so when he did speak to her the conversation would flow.

The conversation would be mostly about interests and not so much the lust he felt in his loins. Like how they both wore glasses, they were the same age, he was taller though they were almost the same height, both in college. She was half Spanish so he knew they both like to dance, and most importantly they were out into the world on their own which was very invigorating. He told himself when he first heard her say hello that he would end up being with her. He knew anyone who saw him with her would automatically know that he was a very lucky guy. From that day anyone could tell that they were going to be close.

They were always chatting each other up and seemed as if they were already a couple. One day he stopped by to get some gum because he was heading out to happy hour. He remembers now because he had on his Perry Ellis outfit which was a chocolate brown long sleeve v-neck shirt, black slacks, and black shoes. All Perry Ellis down.

He knew Adam from working there and Adam told Robert she was new. He went through her line and immediately felt a connection. She was absolutely beautiful. You know men are physical creatures so if there was a radar to detect his attraction from 1 to 10 it would have been on 1000. His very first love at first sight experience.

162

They made small talk before he left the store that day, but he knew he would go back. When he did, they talk more, and she gave him her number. She eventually told him that she hoped he would ask her out the day they actually met. She was just as attracted to him as he was to her. Laughing back at the thought he would almost burst when she told him that about their first encounter. They spent a good amount of time talking and going on dates. It was natural at first, their connection, nothing out of the ordinary yet Robert at 21 was something of a bridled stallion.

He hadn't been intimate for quite some time since his ex who was a school teacher he dated his last year of high school. He didn't want to be immature with Mahogany to pressure being intimate, but he noticed that something stood quite off to him. Things like they had only kissed on the lips once. They were in the park and it started to mist a bit. It was only for a moment, but it was great. It sent more shockwaves through his nerves than had already been. He also noticed that he always kissed her on the cheek when he dropped her off. He was being a gentleman as that is what Mahogany commanded off of the way she carried herself. No way he should have been treating her any differently, but why at that time had he felt as if something was off.

163

They called Mahogany the UNCC version of Hilary Banks, you know the chick that played Will Smith's older female cousin in the TV show The Fresh Prince of Bel-Air. He didn't think she came from that kind of money, but she was a bit high maintenance. You know the way she always had to have dessert with meals, how she never ate fast food, how she had to be...well... perfect when she was out. He found himself going out of his way to treat her the way she wanted even though he was a really simple small-town country boy.

A simple burger, fries, and beer were ideal for him. Mahogany had him at restaurants that he was paying $60-$100 a meal. There was nothing wrong with eating out, but at his age, on a shoe salesman salary he was truly pushing it. No way he should have spent so much on a meal, but he thought you pay for what you want. He also thought maybe he was being used a bit.

See although Mahogany was beautiful, she had bad eyes...like really bad. She would never be able to drive so he was always taking her places and running errands for her. He thought he was doing what a good guy should do. So why does he feel the opposite way? Even took her and her roommate Cali, a slightly larger unattractive woman to places. Doing all of this and not being intimate made him uneasy. He felt they should at least be more intimate, but when he brought it up she kind of blew it off.

By that time he figured it was a breaking point and opted to stop communication with Mahogany. Thinking more about it, it was right around the time he took his friend Tariq, and Tariq's little Tae to the mall to get his ears pierced. He remembers that day because it was the day he met Camille.

Camille worked as the store rep for a place in Carolina Mall called Claire's. Claire's was a store that sold accessories, and they also did piercings. It was a girly store they thought but was the only place to get it done they could think of close to where they stayed. When they walked in he didn't really pay much attention to Camille but as he took notice she stood out more to him. What really got him was her quick wit. He recalled how he asked her if he passed out from getting his ear pierced would she catch him. She told him that the floor would catch him first. For some odd reason, it sparked up something in him, and Mahogany was emotionally fading out of his system.

Camille was another story intimately as she was willing to give him all he wanted and some. He eventually cut off all ties to Mahogany's to start dating Camille. He thought to himself, that was a big mistake. When they say be careful what you ask for, it's completely true. If he knew the hell he would have went through with Camille he would have stayed with Mahogany. Wow! He thought to himself again. The thought sent shivers through his whole body.

He took another sip of Winecoff Vodka sitting outside on his own in his favorite lounge which was Fite's Cigar Bar. He often frequents the place with his childhood friends, but more so by himself. He met Fite, who was from Tennessee while on federal hold for his SEC violation for not filing for exemption which led him to ultimately being sentenced to serve 51 months in federal prison. He did 36 months for good behavior. They talked about Fite opening this bar and was happy his friend did. It was a place he was able to think or even reflect at times. Tonight, was one of those times.

He ran back into Mahogany years later when he returned from Texas and just like before she was still very feminine and commanded the best. They went out just like they had before, but this time they were more intimate. They kissed more on the lips. Progress, but still a slow process. She became a paralegal for a law firm in uptown Charlotte. She was still trying to go to law school. For some reason, she kept taking the bar exam, but not passing.

He shrugged at the thought. He thought of Jenna took a deep breath and sighed at the thought of his friend and attorney. Damn Jenna, he said to himself. She was the reason he was at Fite's drinking in the first place.

Although Mahogany and he got back together he was in no position for a committed relationship. So just like before they just cut ties. Funny how time flies and history repeats itself because it was just about a year later they reconnected again. She was still at the firm and he was starting the promotional aspect of his career. She mentioned how she dated a guy that did all the wrong things. She was out of the dating scene and didn't want a relationship anymore. She just wanted to focus on writing a book in her spare time and passing the bar. He could tell from how she acted that it was a very true statement.

It took persistence to get her to come around but she eventually did fall for him again. He finally was invited over to her apartment one afternoon and it was then he had made love to her. He thought all those years of wanting her so bad, and all the recent efforts he put into wooing her had paid off. He knew it was going to be amazing...probably the best sex he would ever have. Even better than the sex he had with Camille. What it turned out to be was a total disappointment. Not only did she not perform well in the bedroom, but she was

167

also boring. All the passion came from his wanting her and he basically took control the whole time. When it was time for her to be on top she didn't even know what she was doing. When they finished not only did he think it was a bad experience, but he couldn't get over how much hair she had down between her legs. It was like a wild forest he kept saying to himself. How could a woman that beautiful be so bad in bed? Not only that but why did he have so much fucking hair between her legs. When she came back in the room to lay beside him he was disconnected. He later thought it would be better next time...but he was wrong.

He did all the talking as before, the wooing, getting her fired up and about commitment to only sleep with her two more times and still have the same bad experience. He eventually stopped calling and accepting her calls. He went from being madly in love with her to thinking she was just not sexually compatible with him.

He was thinking all of this because he was looking at her again from across the room with some guy. She gained a lot of weight at this point and didn't have the body she had before. Her face was still similar but it was more full. He wondered how many dates they had been on, and if he should reach back out to her. He figured he wouldn't though. May as well let the past be the past.

He then looked down at the cell phone images that were sent to him which presented more pressing issues. How would he deal with this particular situation now that it was brought to his attention? He had a lot of money on the line and had to be smart, yet one thing was certain and two things for sure. Everything with Korina had to immediately stop. These documents were absolute proof of that.

REASON 7

HE'S A CASH COW

───────

There is a saying that refers to women that states "Pussy is Power". If that is the case it should be an alternative energy source...I'm just saying. At any rate, if the vessel of life is as powerful as it truly is then the money is the light switch to a lot of power and as some of the wiser men will instruct younger men to not fall victim to said vagina power. Chase the money not women because women chase the money.

If you're with a guy because you thought he had money, then I need to make aware to you two things. One, he probably left another woman for you. Shame on you, you "home wrecker", and two you will lose him the same way you got him. "That bitch!" Right? Hahaha yet when you are dealing with Cash Cow or CC, you're dealing with one of the most influential characteristics of man on the planet. When that is so you will completely bear witness to just how powerful a vagina can be on a woman who chases CC.

CC does not have to have looks, the body, nor brains for him to cheat. He doesn't even have to be super rich all the same. All CC needs to do is be able to execute financial stability to the less fortunate and it's hasta luego for you. Before you even notice the change, one minute you're in first class drinking champagne with new Louis Vuitton, Burken, or Coach bag...the next minute you're drinking water in the back of coach sitting beside a little league coach with a receding hairline and bad pick up material. Attaboy coach keep at it!

CC cheats because he can basically stabilize the one issue that makes relationships fail. You can assume because of communication or love, and you will make an ass out of you and...you. When CC has more cash than he has personality, looks, swagger, or big weenie; his money talks and there is nowhere in the world women will not listen. Hell, and a lot of cases men too. If you're thinking your hoo-ha got CC tamed baby, think again. CC can go over to an exotic country like Brazil, Costa Rica, The Philippines, Venezuela, or Peru and walk away with a thousand women who look like they just stepped out of a magazine. They will not care about love either. Neither will he because CC will be his own celebrity, and that will place him at the top of the world emotionally.

Most women after dealing with the wrong guys who come across as a CC will go into full commitment status. Heck, I'm not a CC but I remember a woman once saw my house and immediately told me she saw a future with me. We had only been talking for 2 weeks. The night she told me this we went to eat wings and had some drinks. She had to leave for work that morning at 4:30 a.m. we got in at 12 a.m., she told me at 12:30, and we had sex until 3:40 a.m. I know this because I actually timed it, old habits and all.

Do you know that most executives, lawyers, judges, and rich men alike have at least two affairs during their marriage? Almost all of these guys are CCs and the women that they cheat with know he's a cheater and doesn't even care. Some women know CC cheats yet say nothing because they don't want to lose out on their comfortable lifestyle.

Say what you want, but it's true and happens now-a-days more than you think. So, dating CC will is a damned if you do and damned if you don't scenario. If you do, make sure all gifts can be liquidated. I am just saying.

UNUSUAL SUSPECT

The 79th Precinct on Tomkins Ave in Brooklyn was still buzzing with local news reporters who wanted to get more information about any leads on the death of actress Kim Reynolds. It was leaked by a hotel customer that a man was seen coming out of the room the morning she was found dead. Since it was a celebrity that was killed the FBI was called to head the investigation. This did not sit particularly well with Detective Nick Morales who was assigned to the case. Morales was just 6 months away from retirement after being on the force for 30 years. He was one of the detectives from the 79th Precinct that had seen his fair share of drug-dealing scum, pimps, mob figures, and murderers.

The job had taken a toll on his life, his health, from drinking too much, and to his relationship with his wife of 20 years...well, his ex-wife. His ex-wife took his children and moved out to Los Angeles with her therapist. His relationship with his two girls 18, 17, and son 15 were that of a phone call every month every once in a guilt trip blue moon. He knew they were better off with their mom than with him yet he did want to have a relationship with them. The job was very demanding and those who didn't have the balls or moral compass to care about anything other than their self-centered selves can't survive on the job for long. It was a lonely career choice to be passionate about that many never get credit for doing.

It was always a topic in the bar how cops, teachers, military servicemen, women, and firefighters got paid poorly in the United States. The same people who protected, saved, and educated the world got paid less than those they educated. The topic alone made the job more hectic than it was, but Morales like most cops came from a long line of police officers.

His grandfather was on the force, his dad was on the force, his brother was on the force, and his uncle was a retired Detective, so it was destined for him to be as well and in 6 months it will be some other Schmucks problem, a problem that he would not hesitate to turn over.

For now, he needed to find out who was the man at the hotel. The cell phone record led to a Manuel Diaz AKA Domingo who was a tight end for the Miami Dolphins for a couple of years before he became part of Robert Louis's security detail. When he went to the office of Mr. Louis, Mr. Louis was cooperative and was offering all the help he could. A decent guy, Morales thought when he first met him. Morales also checked Diaz's last known address in which he spoke with a Hungarian coked-out bombshell by the name of Natalia Saphowitz.

When asked about the whereabouts of Diaz she said she hadn't seen him since the night in question. He hadn't been back but didn't want him back. Telling from the bruise on her face it seemed he gave her a good reason for her to feel that way. Morales placed a two-man 24-hour surveillance car in front of her residence just in case he came back. He was about to follow up another lead of a sighting from the tip line when he was called into Captain Franklin's office.

Captain Franklin is older than Morales by 5 years and is as hard as nails. Cpt. Franklin played the political circle well and was promoted to the top, and he gave more hell then he did compliments. He reached in his desk drawer to grab two mints to cover the cognac that was on his breath. He made sure it was good then headed to Cpt. Franklin's office.

"Hey Captain, you wanted to see me?

"Yes, Morales come in and shut the door behind you."

Morales closed the door and turned to sit down.

"Remain standing. Where are we with the Kim Reynolds case? I got the commissioner and the Mayor breathing down my neck, and I want this thing off my desk before the election."

At 55 Morales knew he could take his superior who was 60 even though the captain himself was in pretty good shape. The way he talked made Morales want to lay a good one across his ugly mug again. He did it once in the academy, and when Franklin became his superior he made him regret it every single day. Morales told himself he would do it once more for the road.

"I'm following up on the leads from the hotline. We have a unit outside the last known residence, I have subpoenaed his credit cards, but so far he is in the wind.

"So, so far you've got nothing but wasted resources. Is that what you're telling me?"

"No sir I…"

"Shut up Morales. You listen to me and you listen to me well. I didn't want you on this case, but you were all I had close enough to get the job done, so consider this your last chance to make a good impression before you leave. Screw this up and I will throw you out on your ass without a pension."

"Sir with all due respect…"

"Save it, Morales. I knew you would drag ass on this case and now I got the freaking feds all in my yard with this thing. I want it done so you're going to play nice with this agent they sent from Washington."

"What agent?!" Morales bolstered.

Cpt. Franklin leaned toward his right and pointed at a brunette who was standing by Morales's desk.

"That agent," he said. She has been sent to help with this investigation and you damn well better play it fair."

"Captain I don't need an agent to help. I can handle this. I don't need any help."

Cpt. Franklin stood and went to open the door. "It's already settled," he said opening the door and calling the agent over.

"Agent DuBaun" he called.

The brunette walked to his office and entered while remained on his feet.

"Detective Nick Morales this is Special Agent Lindsey DuBaun from the FBI."

She held out her hand and Morales shook it. She had soft hands but a surprisingly strong grip.

"Pleased to meet you," he said.

"Likewise," she responded.

Her eyes were ice blue and her facial features were *model-esque*. She was all legs standing around 5'11 to Morales's 6'2 224 lbs. frame. He pegged her to be around 38 years old, no ring, no widening of hips, or pudge, so he figured no kids. Very attractive...too attractive to be in this line of work. She is probably a lesbian he thought.

"Do we have any updates on the suspect?" she asked looking between the two men commandingly.

Cpt. Franklin looked at Morales with a smug expression knowing this was upsetting him.

"I was just informing the captain I was headed to do a follow-up on a lead from the hotline. A woman from Marcy Projects reported she saw a young guy that looked like the suspect."

"Great let's roll," she said turning to the door walking out.

With DuBaun out the door, Cpt. Franklin told Morales he did not want the FBI taking all the credit for this case even though he knew they would. He ordered Morales to contact him as soon as he had something. Even though he couldn't stand Franklin, Morales felt very much the same when it came to the feds and their jurisdiction. Call it a long-standing feud between the two branches but it seemed every time the bureau guys came in they made a complete mess of things. They treated the uniforms as if they were beneath them.

Morales was a good detective, rough around the edges, but who wouldn't be with this kind of job? You had to be, sometimes 24 hours a day, but it didn't mean he was bad. It was what the job called for at times and he certainly didn't need any uppity suit coming to tell him how to do his job and taking all of the credit. He made a point to be straight to this Agent DuBaun so there would be no misunderstanding. He grabbed his jacket and looked for Agent DuBaun. He walked outside and looked around when he spotted her at a black Dodge Charger.

"Pretty fancy ride you have there."

"It'll get us from point A to point B."

"Better looking than my Crown Vic that's for sure."

"Crowns are classic."

"Yea! Classic pieces of shit" he grinned.

"I figured you wanted me to drive given you may want the cognac to wear off a bit." His grin faded instantly. "By the way, I'm not as enthused about the situation as you so however long or short we seem to be working on this case, I would greatly appreciate it if you don't put our or anyone else's lives in danger. Now let's go."

Morales was instantly furious, and what really threw him over the edge was how she blatantly did so and dismissed him. He could feel his face turning red from his anger rising. He needed to gather his bearings. He reached in his pocket to grab his cigarettes. The window dropped instantly.

"I would also appreciate it if I didn't have the pleasure of smelling smoke while we work together as well. Now if we can go? This case will not solve itself."

He was madder than all hell placing his cigarettes back into his pocket. Getting in the car he almost ripped off the door.

"Look lady!" he screamed. "I don't know what crammed up your crotch but you don't order me around nor do you tell me what to do." He was breathing hard and the stench was stronger.

"Where we going?" she asked.

"Marcy Projects" he responded. She reached in her purse pulled a pack of gum out and threw it in his lap then pulled off.

MARCY PROJECTS

They had to meet with the manager to show them the apartment that Ms. Lillie Mae lived in when they got to the projects. When they arrived at the apartment, the short Creole woman said she saw the man when he was walking into her building. He was talking to a guy name Quiz who Morales knew to be one of the bad in the batch of apples. He was an NGA gang affiliate and was known to carry a firearm. His last known address was just around the corner down the hall. They walked to the door and heard music playing.

Knock! Knock! Knock!

"Who is it?" a female voice said from inside.

Knock! Knock! Knock! "Open up, or we are going to break it down," Morales said.

A young Puerto Rican woman in a silk housecoat opened the door.

"Yes! Can I help you?"

They presented their badges.

"Agent DuBaun and Detective Morales ma'am. We are here regarding an official matter. May we come inside?" Morales said.

181

"What official matter, with who?" the woman said.

"We are looking for Tyree Jackson ma'am have you seen him?" Morales asked.

"Hell no, and I don't want to either."

"Ma'am it may be better if we come inside," Morales said.

She looked back then opened the door further stepping aside. She was around 24 years old, hair up, and in good shape. Morales couldn't help but notice how her nipples protruded through the light blue silk housecoat that hung just short of her thighs.

"When was the last time you saw Mr. Jackson Ms...?"

"Nadia. Nadia Sanchez."

"Ms. Sanchez when was the last time you saw Tyree Jackson?" Morales asked.

"He was here two days ago when we went to the movies but we had to leave early."

"Why is that? DuBaun asked while Morales was looking around.

"He got a call and said we had to go. I waited a month to go to the movies and he breaks it."

"Did he say why?"

"No. We just came back here."

"Then what?"

"Then nothing. We sat, and he left with some guy."

"A guy?" DuBaun said alerted. Morales pulled his cell phone out and presented a picture of Diaz.

"Is it this guy? he asked.

"Yeah, that's him. What did he do?"

"He's a suspect in a homicide."

"Who?"

"Kim Reynolds, the actress," he said.

She sat back. "Son of a bitch."

"Anything else you can tell us? Did he mention where they were going that night?"

"No. No, he didn't."

"Well if you can think of anything please give me a call" Morales pulled his card out and handed it to her. "Do you know of any other places Tyree may hang out at?"

"He may be out at the Rucker. He normally plays ball out there around this time with the guys from the neighborhood."

"Okay, you've been a big help, Ms. Sanchez. If you see Diaz call us as soon as you get the opportunity" Morales said.

"Okay. Damn shame" she said.

"What's that?" Agent DuBaun asked.

"What happened to Kim Reynolds. We were supposed to see The Queen that night."

They turned and walked away.

RUCKER PARK 7:30 p.m.

They pulled up to the corner of Fredrick Douglas Blvd across from the park. There was a game going on as you could hear the trash talkin' from up the street. When they walked down someone started to whistle alerting authorities were near. A couple of people walked off, but the game was so intense Tyree didn't pay any attention to the agent and detective coming his way.

"That's him with the blue sweats and the black and red shoes" Morales pointed out to DuBaun.

Stepping on the court Morales called his name "Tyree Jackson!" Tyree turned and looked.

"Damn it! He's going to run" DuBaun said.

"How do you..." Morales didn't even finish his statement. Tyree bolted to the corner of the court and DuBaun was hot on his trail. Morales went out the same entrance they came in since Tyree ran right out of the court. They could meet at the corner of the street. Morales was just a few steps behind Tyree and DuBaun when he crossed the street towards the Fine Fare Supermarket.

"Stop FBI!" Agent DuBaun shouted.

Tyree just kicked his legs in another gear. Morales caught up with DuBaun. Tyree was throwing over trash cans to slow them down. They diverted them and closed in on him. He was heading full speed to the intersection as cars were coming and he flashed right through making a right into an alley. They were held up by a cab then quickly got around it. When they turned into the alley Tyree was on top of a dumpster reaching for a fire escape.

"Freeze!" Morales drew his sidearm.

Tyree looked then kept climbing. He reached a window then opened it. DuBaun was on the dumpster heading the same way. Morales checked the door entering the building but it was locked. He took a step back and threw his left shoulder into it bursting it open. DuBaun cleared the dumpster when she stuck her head in the window that entered the room of a shop that had headless mannequins, fabrics, sewing machines and rolls of thread.

The shop was well-lit, so she could see that the door was shutting where Tyree recently exited. She sprinted to the door, drew her weapon, checked, and just caught Tyree making a right down the hall.DuBuan was in full sprint and she turned the right corner. The door to the staircase was hitting the wall and she could see Tyree heading up the staircase just to the left.

"Freeze FBI!" she yelled going up two stairs at a time. He was just a staircase ahead. Tyree got up to the third floor and checked the door, but it was locked. He continued up to the 4th. He tried to open the door to his right, but it was locked. He took off further down the hall as he saw the female agent coming through the door from the staircase. He saw the exit to the staircase again. He checked the door to the right and it was open, so he rushed in and locked it.

The whole floor was open, so he rushed to the window to get back to the outside stairwell. Morales was just opening the door from the basement when he cut down the hall to see the main lobby undisturbed.

"Where are your stairs?!" he yelled to the front desk clerk.

She pointed to a door just to his left. He opened the door to see DuBaun chasing Tyree up to the 4th floor. He sprinted as fast as he could, his heart beating hard against his chest. His lungs were burning. He told himself he needed to stop smoking. Making up time with four steps at a time he made it to the 4th floor. Morales saw DuBuan had just entered a door from where he was at the end of the hall. Damn, she's fast. He got to the door and saw nothing as he entered. He looked around. "Where the hell did they?"...he saw the window. He stuck his head out the window and saw they were at the bottom of the staircase. He jumped on the stairs, sliding down halfway per rail section.

Agent DuBaun was in the middle of the street when he hit the asphalt. They made a right on the street going towards some Asian restaurants. Tyree was knocking into people as he went through the crowd. There was a delivery bike that came out of nowhere that he barely missed, and when he dodged to the left DuBaun tackled him. They were rolled, but she didn't have him secure, and he was back into the restaurant. He ran to the kitchen, and out the back into an alley. Morales helped DuBaun up and they were back in pursuit.

Once they went out the back of the restaurant Tyree was gone. They split up. DuBaun went left and Morales went right. Morales drew his gun again. He was trying to control his breathing. His palms were sweaty, and his heart felt as if it was going to beat out of his chest. He thought something moved to his left, so he swung his Glock in the direction. It was some large rats piled around some trash. He focused back toward the alley as he walked slowly down, then two shots rang out. He ran back into the direction DuBaun was to see her standing over Jackson's body.

"What happened?" Morales kneeled checking Jackson's pulse.

"He had a knife and charged. I was lucky I saw it in time."

Morales noticed the small blade in the man's handgrip. He also noticed that Tyree had a faint heartbeat. He wouldn't have long to live so Morales radioed a bus. When they got Tyree to the hospital he had lost a lot of blood and was in a critical condition but he was going to make it. He was in a coma and doctors didn't give him a big chance of surviving, but he did have a chance. Morales and DuBuan would use that chance to question him to find out where Diaz was.

79th PRECINCT BROOKLYN

Back at the station Morales filed the field report and DuBaun called her superior as well, who was not happy she nearly killed the only possible good lead they had. When she got off the phone Morales could almost feel the same emotion come out of her system. He wasn't a rookie to being scorned from his superiors or the media for that matter. He thought he may as well play nice since it was late, so he reached in his desk and pulled out two paper cups with a bottle of Victor O'Neill.

She just looked at him as he poured with what seemed like disgust. He pushed a cup towards her. She eyed the cup with a somber deep breath, then got up and walked off. He took a cup then thought to himself the lesbian must not like cognac. Halfway through his cup, she reemerged with a bottle of vodka. He sat back admiring her while she poured the second cup into his cup then poured her vodka in the second cup. She took a big gulp then poured another.

"So, what's your story?" Morales asked as she started to settle in the seat across from him.

"Long or short version?"

"Short."

She took a drink then proceeded to tell him how she was from out Midwest. She wanted to be a model because she loved modeling. Her father who was a bad gambler and a mill worker couldn't afford it, so she joined the military. She was on her second tour when she met a guy that she ended up marrying and was deployed back in the states.

Life was good, but her dad got in with some bad people and was murdered. She went to school, graduated 25th in her class, and set out head first into law enforcement at the bureau. She wanted to know who murdered her dad but when she dug deeper they killed her husband. She was even attacked herself.

Not stopping she made some connections and figured she would be able to do more with the bureau's help. She also has three half-brothers that she wasn't too close to because her father had an affair with her mom. She was pregnant when she was attacked and lost the baby. She has been focused on work ever since. Morales couldn't help but think he was a schmuck for treating her the way he did and calling her a lesbian. To himself, he apologized to her. They sat in silence for a moment then the phone at his desk rang.

"Detective Morales."

He sat quietly for a second then spoke agreeing.

"Thank you for letting me know," he said then hung up the phone. "That was the hospital," he said looking at DuBaun. She sat up in her seat. "Tyree didn't make it" he said. They just sat with the bottles between them. Back to square one.

FAR ROCKAWAY LONG ISLAND

—————

The next morning Morales had a slight hangover which he immediately cured with a triple shot of cognac. By the time he was dressed he had a buzz that would take him through lunch. Yet he was puzzled about something given how everything came about after the shooting. Pondering on it a minute he figured it would come to him. The apartment he had wasn't much, but it was decent for his salary. There wasn't much of a Feng Shui with the basic tan carpet, brown sofa, loveseat, end tables, coffee table, and entertainment system. It looked like something out of a Rooms-To-Go ad along with his bedroom and two spare rooms. All of it was, and to him, if it was good enough for the ad it was good enough for him.

As he fixed his tie, he smelled bacon coming from the kitchen. Looking himself over once more; splashed a bit of Alfred Hei on and headed toward the kitchen.

"Smells good in here," he said heading to the coffee machine. He poured himself a mug then sat at the table beside the newspaper.

"You're on the cover of that you know?"

"Oh yeah?"

"Yeah! And you look like hell, but in a good kind of way."

"I felt like hell. I haven't run like that in ages."

"It showed. You were out like a light after we finished last night. You snored so hard I got up and slept in the spare bedroom."

"I don't snore."

"Honey you do more than snore. You call the hogs."

"Leave it to you to mention something about hogs you country bumpkin."

"Country bumpkin?" she turned with plates of bacon, eggs, and toast.

She set the plates on the table then got to the pot of grits, poured them into two separate bowls then placed them on the table.

"You didn't say that last night now did you?"

She placed a kiss on his forehead and he slapped her playfully on the rear. She sat across from him and started to eat, and she watched him do the same, as he bit into his toast.

"So?"

"So what?"

"How was Agent DuBaun?"

"She seems to be like all the other suits." he said.

"I mean is she nice? Is she dedicated to the job?"

"You mean is she pretty?"

"Hey, you said it not me."

"But you're wondering."

"I already know she is attractive Nick; I mean she has to be."

"Why do you say that?" he asked.

"A woman knows Nick and you did a lot of confirming when you got here this morning."

"How do you know?" he asked looking at her.

"Because of the way we had sex last night. It was different. We have sex and it's good, but a woman can tell when her man is having sex with her or someone else."

"I'm not cheating on you."

"I didn't say you were cheating, I said you were having sex with someone else."

"That doesn't make sense. How can I not cheat but have sex with another woman?"

"Because even though you were with me you were sleeping with that Agent."

"That sounds crazy," he said.

"Call it what you want but I was her last night. Don't get me wrong I didn't mind as long as I was her and she wasn't."

He looked at her puzzled, but he knew she was dead on the money. He had done it often, yet he figured it wasn't a big deal so what's the harm? It wasn't as if they were exclusive or anything. They just got together here and there, and he would help her financially from time to time. He met Marlene when his unit raided a home for drugs and her boyfriend went to jail. She was a hot little number from Bennettsville, South Carolina that moved to the big city. She got with the wrong kind of guy and could use a hand every now and again. She was in her thirties with three kids and was doing what she could to get back on her feet.

After the raid he saw her at a market and things just went from there. Her being around made the place less depressive along with him not feeling so alone. Ever since his divorce with Catherine life seemed to take on a darker meaning. He drank more to the point it was mentioned he needed counseling. He considered it before but fell out with the sponsor so he stopped attending.

Marlene fit his life at the moment and for the moment was all right with him. He didn't even mind that she had kids as he inconveniently met them while out at the market. Nice group of kids although the son seemed he would be in cuffs by 16. He just had a really bad aura to him and she babied it. That was part of the reason he never fully committed.

"You wasn't her, you were you because if you were the agent, you wouldn't have a key to my place nor be making bacon in my kitchen. This is good by the way" he said taking a bite.

"Thank you liar" she smirked.

"You were great by the way. I needed that."

"You're welcome and I know," she said grinning.

"Will you be here when I get off tonight?" he asked.

"I can if you want me to be. My friend is at my place for a couple of days, so she will watch them."

"Must be kind of tight on space."

"We'll manage till we figure something out for her."

Morales immediately wanted to change the subject because he knew where this was going. He was not in

197

the mood nor did he have an interest in what was to come. He reached in his wallet and gave her $200.

"Here take this and grab some groceries. I'm sure with more people in the house it's depleting the fridge plus I want you to have all the energy you can for the next time we get together." Hopefully, he saved that from sounding so degrading towards her.

"You don't have to," she said.

"It's nothing. Plus, the more comfortable you are the less stressed you are, which leads to a happier you."

He thought for a moment then told her he wanted her to gather all her bills and they would sit down together to come up with a solid plan to get them caught up, plus help her with her credit. This lit a fire in Marleen and she almost started crying. She hugged and kissed him passionately. When he left he thought maybe he shouldn't have done that but it was already said so he would keep his word. He was walking to his car when his phone rang. It was agent DuBaun. What she told him made his whole body turned cold.

"I'll be right there," he said and hung up the phone.

NADIA SANCHEZ APARTMENT

When Morales pulled up to the towers there was a group of NGA members, and other patrons at the tower entrance. There were police officers at the door, showing his badge they allowed him up. He got on the elevator and went to the 6th floor. Making a right off the elevator he could see residents standing outside of their apartments looking towards Nadia's. There was a group of uniforms standing at the door with caution tape. He approached showing his badge when DuBaun said from inside "Let him in."

He cleared the tape to walk through the door to see the forensics team taking pictures of two female bodies.

"Jesus!" he said out loud.

He was looking at Nadia Sanchez and Natalia Saphowitz with gunshot wounds to the chest and their faces cut to the corners of their mouths.

"What happened?" Morales said.

"Neighbors said that they heard an altercation between the two women. A moment later all hell broke loose and that's when they heard the shots" DuBaun said.

"Did anyone see anything?"

"They say they didn't but there were plenty of people in the courtyard."

"So, they saw but they're not talking?"

"Yes, pretty much."

"Did they mention when or what time the shots happened?"

"Early this morning around 6 a.m. is when the neighbors heard all the arguing."

"This doesn't look like a regular girl fight DuBaun." Morales said.

"I know it doesn't. As soon as I saw their faces I knew it was a hit. Someone lured Natalia over here to get them in the same place. I mean why else would she be here?"

"I think you may be halfway right," Morales said.

"Why is that? DuBaun asked.

"The mob of Tyree's friends outside says it's retaliation for him."

"You don't think..." DuBaun started to speak.

"Yes. Someone saw us talk to them and after Tyree was killed they killed them both."

"Do you think it leads to Diaz?" she asked.

"It could, as he has strong ties to the NGA and it would be a great smokescreen," Morales said.

"But why create a bigger target for yourself when authorities are already pegging you for a high-profile homicide? He couldn't possibly think killing more people would change our course."

"Penny for your thoughts," Morales asked.

"Two," she said.

"I think Diaz has something to do with this, but I'm not counting out a puppet master."

"So you think someone else is calling the shots on this?"

"Yes, I do."

"But who will go through all this trouble and why?" DuBaun asked.

"Now that is the right question."

"Here is another question then. Where do we go from here?" DuBaun asked.

Morales kneeled and bagged two different shell casings." Do you have a nice dress?"

Agent DuBaun looked at him mysteriously. "We need to go to the club." Her head leaned to one side in curiosity.

PURE LOUNGE

DuBaun and Morales arrived separately but met in the front of the highly energetic lounge. Its onyx black sign lit up in thin Impact font. This made the lounge presence look so sophisticated. The outside had a red-carpet line that was full of cocktail dresses, heels, and tailored suits. The talk of most was that Milan Italy's own EDM heart throb DJ Alex Guesta had been flown in to exclusively gig for the evening. Alex Guesta was huge in the European circuit with the likes of famed group Swedish House Mafia. Alex brought something special to the EDM world of DJing. He not only spun records, but he was also a drummer and played in his set which was extremely appealing given no one else was doing it. Alex would pull out his sticks and people danced to his rhythmic sounds. He was adored by women too as he would hand them flowers during his set.

Morales wore a shirt and suit by Dolce & Gabbana, tie by Gitman Bros., and shoes by Grensen. It was all navy blue but fitting. He wouldn't have dared spent the money he did had it not been for Marleen who but all told him he would need to look the part for this particular night. Although it was way out of his budget he couldn't help but admire himself. When he saw Agent DuBaun she looked as if she belonged to this crowd. The woman was all legs and gorgeous. She wore a black shimmering Noble Society spaghetti strap thigh-length dress with matching heels. She was breathtaking he thought. Her hair was in a bang bump with the rest pulled in a long ponytail. Her earrings were long and matched her dress. She could definitely have been a runway model.

"You were right!"

"About what?"

"You were into modeling. You look like one of these people."

"What people is that?" she asked.

"You know one of these beautiful people," he said fidgeting. He was blushing, and she noticed.

"Oh well, you clean up well yourself." A moment of awkward silence passed.

"So what are we doing here of all places?" DuBaun asked breaking the silence.

"We were invited."

"By who?"

"Mr. Louis."

"When?"

"When he said he was willing to help in any way he could with this investigation."

"Okay not to sound rhetorical but how does this help?"

"Mr. Louis and his staff were the closest to Diaz and Kim Reynolds. Figured we could come and ask a few questions to see if we get anything."

"So you figure we come out on a packed night like this? No one will talk to us."

"Not comfortably they won't, but in a rush, they may and maybe that will give us the leverage we need."

"Okay let's go."

Passing the line, they showed their credentials Morales told the bouncer they were personal guests of Mr. Louis. The bouncer checked the list then whispered into his wrist. Placing a finger to his ear, he then removed the velvet separator allowing them through. They tried to walk straight through the red carpet, but photographers were shouting for them to pose and comment. He felt a bit important as he walked through hand behind the back of Agent DuBaun escorting her through. Once at the main entrance they were greeted by an Asian hostess who said Mr. Louis had a table set for them and he would be down shortly. They looked at each other then followed. Seeing no sense in waiting Morales started with the beautiful Asian.

"So where is Mr. Louis?"

"There in his office" she pointed her finger to the long strip of mirrored glass on the third floor.

"Pretty good view from up there," he said to DuBaun.

"Do you know his security pretty well?" Morales asked.

"Sure. Everyone knows those guys. People often come here to get their autographs."

"Really?"

"Sure. It's another way to keep people coming to the lounge. Mr. Louis is a very effective marketer."

"Yeah and too efficient if you ask me," he said to DuBaun.

"How is his security with the rest of the employees?"

"How do you mean?" she asked.

"Do they get along?"

"For the most part, they do. I mean they are his security, so they are a bit edgy but outside of that they are pretty cool."

"Anyone have any issues with any of them?"

"No, not that I can recall. Here we are" she showed them a table that was on the second floor to the backside of the lounge. Not the most perfect table but it was a good enough view.

"Mr. Louis says he will be down shortly and all drinks are on the house. Can I start you off with anything?" she asked.

"Double Victor O'Neil" Morales ordered.

"Apple martini," DuBaun said.

"Sure thing" and she left.

"I truly hope nothing happens tonight," Morales said.

"What do you mean like solve this case?"

"Yes!"

"Why in the world would you say something so insane like that? Forget it don't even answer that" she said.

"I say that because moments like this never happened to guys like me. This environment, this kind of lavish life is what guys like me dream of...well used to anyway." She just looked at him. "I think if I could have been this kind of guy maybe my wife would have stayed. I just...you know?" Morales looked off to the side.

DuBaun could see the pain in his eyes and could see that he genuinely was a good guy. "Yeah I actually do but we swore an oath you know so we only get this life at this moment. One thing we can do is drink like it anyway" she said smiling at him.

"Hell yeah," he grunted.

Their drinks were returned by a Latin male in his early 20s.

"Hey! What happened to the young lady that brought us in?" DuBaun asked.

"She was just your table host for this section. I'm Chaz your actual server for this evening" he handed them their drinks. "Can I get you anything else?" he asked.

"Sure, how about some info on one of Mr. Louis's security detail?"

"Sure, but I don't know how much help I'll be."

"Why is that?" DuBaun asked.

"Because I've only been here a week. The only one I know of that can help with Mr. Louis's security is the club manager Mr. Lynn."

"You mean Michael Lynn?" Morales asked.

"Yes, he handles all the hiring for Mr. Louis."

"Is he here?"

"Sure he's right over there…front table VIP next to the DJ booth" Chaz walked off.

207

"Who is Michael Lynn?" DuBaun asked.

Morales pointed at the man in all black with the cold facial expression. "Michael Lynn is Mr. Louis's older brother. He is also the poster child for mayhem. Got a rap sheet about as long as my left leg. Real no sense kind of guy. He once threw a guy out of a two-story window because he thought the guy was staring at him."

"Staring?!"

"Yes staring."

"Well, that alone warrants an invitation for introduction in my book," DuBaun said.

"Got your gun?" Morales asked.

"Yes," she responded.

He looked at her curiously up and down in the fitting dress.

"Oh yeah!" he said excitedly. "Let's go." He sat down his drink as did she, and they headed to Mr. Lynn's section.

Mr. Lynn was accompanied by 4 women who looked like models from hip hop videos. Two Asians, one Spanish, and one Caucasian. There were also two other unsavory men with him as well. One is a known pioneer of the Tre Eight Wolf line of NGA by the name of Delmont Miller aka Nation who was extremely militant.

"Shit we are just in all the great shit of company tonight," DuBaun said.

"Old friend of yours?" Morales said.

"Not him but the other one."

"Oh yeah? Who is he?"

"LeTrais 'The Reaper' Roseman. He's your description of Lynn, but with explosives and combat experience as a warm and cuddly side. The FBI was after him for the death of a foreign national but couldn't touch him."

"Jesus, how the hell did I get this case?" Morales said.

"I don't know but if there was a point when things got bad this would be one of the shit is about to hit the fan types."

"Shit I just got this damn suit," Morales said.

"Excuse me, Mr. Lynn. Detective Morales and Special Agent DuBaun of the FBI. May we have a moment of your time?" Morales said while he and DuBaun exposed their badges. He looked at them annoyed and gave the security guard a cold expression then nodded. The security guard allowed them to pass.

"What can I do for you Detective, and what was it again?" he asked looking at DuBaun.

"Special Agent Lindsay DuBaun FBI" DuBaun reiterated.

"Oooooo Agent DuBaun FBI," he said mockingly. I am most pleased to make your acquaintance" he laughed with the other men. "I wasn't aware that the FBI had such beautiful agents. You must excuse me for being so taken by your beauty. Please have a seat." He nodded his head to the white model and she moved out of the way to make some space for DuBaun to sit next to him.

"No thank you I will remain standing as this will not take long."

"What a pity as I was in the mood to take all the time in the world with you. Perhaps some other time then" he laughed again with the group.

"DuBaun could feel herself tensing the edge of overreaction. Morales chimed in.

"We would like to ask you about one of your employees...a Manuel Domingo Diaz." All the men appeared unshaken at the question but DuBaun could tell it rattled them a little.

"I haven't seen him in weeks. He hasn't called to tell me he needed a leave of absence." he and the others laughed again.

"I'm sure this is all funny to you but I'm sure the family of the woman he killed along with America doesn't," DuBaun said sternly.

"Only person here who recently killed someone lately is you Agent DuBaun," Nation said angrily.

"Oooooo tisk tisk now," Lynn said mockingly.

"You killed my people in cold blood bitch. You got some nerve showing your face around here."

"Bitch?" DuBaun said questionably. "Now that is such an intelligent word coming from you. I'll make sure I thank your mama for being a great example of what she raised you to be" she said snappily.

"Hahahaha" Morales sarcastically chuckled.

Nation started to raise and Morales and DuBaun stepped closer. Mr. Lynn placed his hand on Nations arms stopping him immediately.

"Not here" Nation reluctantly set back in his chair.

"As amusing as this will sound to you officers; truth is I'm sure I can't be of any help as I do not know where Domingo is but if I happen to run into him I will pass along your concerns to communicate with him urgently. Now if you don't mind, since you will not be joining us, would you extend the professional courtesy of allowing us to enjoy the rest of our evening without further conflict" Mr. Lynn said.

A low calm cool voice came from behind the officers. "That sounds like a great idea, why don't you and your friends find another section while you're at it as this one is no longer available". They all turned around to see Robert Louis with his security.

Lynn looked at his brother then looked around. "Come on ladies allow me to show you the rest of the hottest lounge on the East Coast, gentlemen," he said. He stood extending his arm for passage of his company. They all immediately stood up and started to leave. "Enjoy the rest of your evening officers" Lynn said as he walked off with the Asian model on his arm.

DuBaun looked at LeTrais speak into the ear of Nation and smirk while looking at her. Morales could see the blood rushing to her face...hands clenched.

"When I extended my hospitality to you I thought it would be taken as a moment to relax not to interrogate my employees. Had I known you wanted to do so I would have scheduled a day for you to do so." Robert Louis was still a gentleman, but his tone was eerily cold and irritated.

"Excuse me, Mr. Louis, my apologies, it's an occupational hazard."

212

"Very well, I understand completely. Kim was a good friend of mine and no one wants to see her life result in proper justice than I, but I must request it not be at the expense of citizens who are trying to enjoy their evenings or earn an honest living."

"We absolutely agree and thank you again for your generous hospitality," DuBaun said.

"Well then I shall leave you to enjoy the rest of your evening." he shook Morales's hand. As he took DuBaun's hand he covered it with his other hand. "We hadn't the pleasure of being properly introduced Agent DuBaun, but I hope that if you need anything at all you would give me a call, and may I say you look absolutely ravishing this evening."

"Thank you, Mr. Louis. Your hospitality has been most kind and we thank you for all your help in this matter. We shall catch the culprit who is responsible for such a terrible act." she placed her hand on top of his. He nodded genuinely as if to hold back tears that may have been burning the back of his eyes.

"Well then please enjoy the rest of your evening."

As he started to walk off Morales said, "Sorry to be a thorn in the heel but how about tomorrow?"

"Sir?" he turned questionably at Morales.

"Well, you mentioned you would set a day aside for us to speak with your employees. Figured we would get it out of the way so we wouldn't have to show up during business hours and all."

"Mr. Louis looked at his security for a second then said "Sure. Please confirm with my assistant and she will have everyone ready for you. Now if you excuse me I need to go shake my proverbial tin cup at Ms. Patton over there." He nodded and walked off with the wall of well-dressed men in black concealing him.

"The hand thing was a nice touch. They teach that at the bureau?"

"No. That comes from being a woman."

"Guy about lost it for a second even had me all mushy inside."

"Well, he lost someone dear to him how would you expect him to respond?" DuBaun said.

"Yeah I guess so," he said.

"Well, we didn't make friends with his brother and those thugs. I'm sure they don't feel all tingly about us either" DuBaun said.

"Yeah, we will need to watch ourselves with those two, but my question is if Mr. Louis runs such a tight ship he couldn't have missed those two."

"I thought about that as well. Did you see how they responded to him when he showed up? They didn't even make eye contact."

"Yeah he was as an un-American Idol with them," Morales said.

"Something's there Morales. I can feel it" DuBaun said shaking her head.

"Well, we can feel it tomorrow when we come to shake up the place. Until then, do you want to grab a drink and watch the show?" Morales asked.

"I wouldn't dream of wasting this dress on a hanger at this moment. Plus, I'm a fan of Alex Guesta" she smiled.

They made their way back to their VIP table just as a camera took photos of them and another elder male with his companion.

FAR ROCKAWAY LONG ISLAND

W hen Morales got home he was good and wasted like he had been so many nights. He had a slight stagger but was somewhat maintaining to get through his living room. He laid his key on the nightstand and noticed Marleen's keys. He thought of DuBaun in the sleek black dress and heels. He could see her look over her shoulder at him and lift her dress exposing her ass and a black thong. He blinked, and she smiled at him.

He walked into his bedroom and opened the door. Marleen was lying with her back turned to him. He could see the thin sheet running along her frame. He took off his clothes right at the door breathing hard. He was getting aroused as he saw Dubaun turn facing him, lifting her dress over her head still in her heels and thong.

She didn't hear the two men come upon her as she got out of her car. They hit her fast and hard. She turned to see them masked as one punched her in the jaw, slamming her head against the top of the door. She tried to reach to her thigh strap where she concealed a baby .380, but one of the men heeled her in the forehead. She fell back and one of the men grabbed her gun. He slid the gun under the car to the right. She could see it as about four cars over, well out of reach. They were at her feet while her head was at the concrete wall. She couldn't escape.

Morales pulled the covers from over Marleen body which exposed her in a white t-shirt with white underwear. Her eyes opened, she could smell the alcohol on him, and she could hear him breathing hard. He climbed on the bed and laid behind her back.

"No!" She screamed as one of the men kicked her between the legs. She folded in pain as the men continued to kick her in the back, ribs, and butt. One kneeled and punched her right in the ear making her head hit the concrete floor. She tried her best to stand and lunge to run but as soon as she did one of the men punched her in the mouth. She could feel a tooth fly into her jaw and one on the bottom bend back toward her tongue. The man behind her put her in a chokehold. She tried to breathe as blood swelled in her head almost turning her face purple.

Morales looked at DuBaun's back as she bent over and slid down her thong. He stroked himself a couple of times and pulled down Marleen's underwear. He lifted her right butt cheek and found her vagina with his middle finger. He slid it in and she was already wet. He rubbed her juice on the top of his penis and slid his penis in

217

thrusting it in real hard. It made Marleen tighten and try to push his waist backward.

DuBaun tried to scream but she couldn't open her mouth as the man large arm was around her throat. She clawed at the masked beast as much as she could but couldn't get a grip. The man standing in front of her kicked her again between the legs sending a sharp pain into her stomach. Blood started to run down her inner thigh. It felt warm against her skin.

The man behind her was breathing hard. He let her loose enough to turn around and head butt her in the nose. As she fell he held onto her dress ripping right down the middle until it was just a piece of rag. She had red bruises all over and blood was oozing from her face. Her mouth had swollen as well as her left eye. "Pweeze don't!" she begged as one of the men slapped her.

As Morales moved deeper into DuBaun she placed her arm behind his neck. He moaned with passion and she became moist. He stuck his finger in her mouth and started to stroke her harder and faster. Marleen's body jolted with every connection of Morales's pelvic thrust to her ass. It sounded like it was being smacked. She rubbed her tongue around his finger and sucked on it as if It was his penis.

"Aaagghh!" one of the men said as he entered DuBaun. He grunted as he stroked her a second time. He started to climax as he stroked her four more times. His body convulsed as he stroked one more time for measure and collapsed on her. He stood, and semen and blood dripped from his penis. DuBaun's body started to shake uncontrollably. "Nah bitch, don't get scared now," the other man said as he was stroking himself. "Turn that bitch over" he said. The other man kicked her in the ribs breaking them and she felt the excruciating pain. He rolled her over on the stomach. Still stroking inside her, he grabbed her by the hair with his left hand and begin to pound her hard from the back.

"Yes!" DuBaun said to him. "Harder! Harder!" she said to Morales. He was breathing heavily, and Marlene just lifted her butt, so he could go deeper into her. He started to climax which made her moan out loud, turning on Morales even more.

DuBaun couldn't speak, she could only feel the sharp pain in her rectum that felt like a tear as the man entered her anus. Her body moved up and down mechanically. Everything was silent with only one eye slightly open she saw her husband reaching his hand to her under the car. She gave the best effort she could to reach him. Her body still rocking up and down, silent but existing. He reached to her mouthing "Take my hand. Take my hand. I love you".

Morales climaxed deep into DuBaun as she laid in complete bliss with a smile on her face. Marleen had sweat coming from her forehead as she laid with Morales still semi-erect inside of her. She could feel his penis pulsating slowly as It was getting slower and slower.

Her fingers were just about to reach her husband's when a gunshot exploded into her back. The vision of her husband started fading black and he was still mouthing "I love you" when another shot collapsed in her back.

Marleen could no longer feel the pulsation as she fell asleep.

REASON EIGHT

HE'S A SUGAR DADDY

As self-explanatory as my number eight example maybe let's just be completely honest here. If you ever had a chance to be with Sugar Daddy, then you good and damn well knew what the heck he was, no two ways about it.

Don't give some excuse as to why you did not because yes you did. Tell yourself "Self. Yes, I did." If you are in denial about knowing good and well your agenda with a sugar daddy, then you my dear friend are the most fibbing person on the planet. I'm going to get you a t-shirt that has "Fibber Fibber Chicken Weenie" on the front.

You should be completely ashamed of committing such a monstrosity of a lie. Who do you think you're fooling? Do you know the higher power does not like ugly? Yet you're going to sit here, read this book, and truly concede to such blasphemy. Ha! You should be punished for such an act.

You should be filled with water, made to sit for 6 hours, and tickled until you have not one tear in your eye. I would ask you to prove it. It will come back to haunt you

221

and when it does I will send my tickle squad to chain you down, remove your shoes, and tickle you until you have stomach cramps. Make you beg for mercy you fibber fibber chicken weenie. What am I, 5 with that line? Ha!

Anyway, Sugar Daddy is probably the only cheater you don't experience true heartbreak from. Hell, if anything you are disappointed you forgot to take advantage of obtaining something while you had Sugar Daddy's attention. Yet let's explore the depths of Sugar Daddy because although you may see the physical and financial consciousness you don't see the multiplicity cognitive about him.

One thing you need to consume about Sugar Daddy is that he has no real intention of committing to you. He only commits to the fantasy of you. He likes the fact that he can control with financial stability while avoiding the alternative responsibility he has elsewhere. Sugar Daddy looks for a living, breathing, do it all toy. No different than the multi-million-dollar collection of toys in the garage, jewelry box, closet, or packed in airline miles to exotic locations. Sugar Daddy feeds off the void of the absentee daddy issue which can be extremely dangerous as much as it is mentally abusive. This life of the lavish Casanova will have you wishing long after he bid you the ultimate farewell because he is rare to come by which makes your commitment to him so much more vulnerable.

Now your other issue with Sugar Daddy is that other women also see him as a meal ticket. Believe it or not more women are the initiators that cause the heartbreak of men. Been that way since the beginning of man. Remember Eve? Pow! I had to say that it was starting to give me a headache.

Sugar Daddy is a conqueror no doubt about it as he takes on many forms. One that we will explain later is just too unavoidable. Sugar daddy is bored at home and there is some young hot college type that is willing to allow him to explore all his sexual fantasies of a youthful woman that his older, respectable self wouldn't get to experience. Again, just like the case with CC, the woman is just as responsible as he is. It's your feelings or her college tuition, bills, or stability and guess who is going to lose? She will have planned or beckoning calls with a sugar daddy. He will fall knee-deep in not only the act of sleeping with someone younger, perkier, tighter, energetic, and moist than you. He will also have the unconscious sick thought of having sex with someone his daughter's age. Yes, make no mistake about it. Sugar Daddy is just not a pervert he is damn near a pedophile. The sad thing is some parents will allow such a relationship "Hoooooollywood chew!

223

Hoooooollywood chew!" Excuse me. My allergies are acting up.

It's hard to keep Sugar Daddy in a bitter black coffee mood. Again many women will allow such a relationship because they don't want to lose out on the financial stability he can provide. If you are with a Sugar Daddy and you know, then as the saying goes game recognize game. Yet if you do end up catching feelings for Sugar Daddy or know your husband or currently in a relationship with one. My dear grab some big condoms and put them over your heart because just like you are having sex for money sugar daddy is going to fuck your feelings when it's over...on to the next one.

GIFT OF ROSES

"Happy Birthday to you! Happy Birthday to you! Happy Birthday dear Kayla, Happy Birthday to you!"

"Can I help blow out the candles?" Brady asked full of excitement.

"Sure! You can help Kayla" responded.

"Neato!"

"On 3 okay?"

"Okay."

"1...2...3 blow" Kayla and Brady blew the 18 candles out on the cake for her 18th birthday.

Sheila had a few of her close friends from school and other families who came to visit at the house for a small gathering. Kayla was so excited about today because it meant so much. It meant she could buy cigarettes, even though she didn't smoke. It meant she could get into R-rated films legally even though she had done so before anyway. It meant she could get into clubs, although she had done that as well. But most importantly it meant she was technically an adult. She can move out on her own and conquer the world, and no one could stop her.

"What did you wish for Kayla?" Brady asked.

"Not supposed to say, bro. It's bad luck and may not come true." "That's right" Sheila chimed in. "How about some cake everyone?"

Of course, Brady was at the table ready with his plate. A lot changed with their family and they were trying to get back on their feet. Sheila found out that Dan was at a hotel with another woman when pictures surfaced around Kayla's school of some of her friends. When Kayla looked closer she noticed Dan in the background. She showed her mom and they had a big argument because it was of him and a woman Dan promised he would never communicate with. Sheila took money out of her 401k to help fund Dan's GCB project, but now she had to use it for the medical treatment she needed. With Dan out of the picture, money was tight and Sheila was going to barely be able to send Kayla to college.

The party was still in gear with Kayla's friends when all started to adore the necklace that Kaitlyn was wearing. It was an all diamond necklace from Tiffany's.

"Wow that's beautiful," Taylor said.

"Thanks, babes" Kaitlyn responded.

"It looks like it costs a fortune," Kayla said.

"It was a gift, but it is the best right?" Kaitlyn said playing with the necklace.

"Oh sure," Stephanie agreed.

"So...you care to fill us in or are you going to keep it all a secret?" Taylor asked questionably.

"I'm going to keep it a secret," Kaitlyn said.

"Keep what a secret?" Kayla asked.

"You're bday prez," Taylor said.

"It's nothing really, I just wanted to do something special for you and what a better day to do something special on? I mean you're only 18 once right?" Kaitlyn said.

"So, what is it?" Kayla asked.

"You'll see, we just need to wait until everyone leaves."

It wasn't until everyone left and Sheila went to bed when the girls began to get dressed in some very provocative clothing. Kaitlyn handed Kayla a bag from Louis Vuitton with a beautiful fitting red dress.

"Holy shit! Kaitlyn, I don't know what to say. I've never had anything like this before. Thank you so much" she hugged her friend.

"Put it on. It's the same one Zendaya had on when she went to the Met Gala."

Kaitlyn looked at Taylor and Taylor looked back at Kaitlyn with a devious grin. When Kayla put on the dress she looked as if she was much older than her 18 years. She admired herself in the mirror thinking this is the type of dress that she wanted to be able to buy when she was older. She wanted to attend really important parties with really important people because she would be famous. She wanted to be able to do more for her mom and brother since her dad left and started a new family. She figured if she was important people would notice her and like her more.

She was doing all she could at the moment to hang with Taylor, Stephanie, Kaitlyn, and Mecca. They were all gorgeous girls from prominent families. They took her in when she first came to their school. In the beginning, they were sort of mean, but when her mom started dating Dan people noticed her more. They invited her to parties at their homes and even Jason Mullins noticed her and asked her out. All of that was okay, but they stumbled on a way to make some money and she looked forward to making some on her own now that she was 18 years old. Kaitlyn and Taylor had done so, and they both were doing all right.

Once all the girls were dressed they took selfies and snuck out of the house. There was a limo waiting for them outside that didn't put the lights on until they got out of the door.

"Where are we going?" Kayla asked.

"Mecca got us into Pure Lounge," Kaitlyn said.

"No way. That's the hottest lounge around. How did that happen?"

"Her guy is a dynasty, so he gets in with whomever he wants no questions asked," Kaitlyn said.

"What's a dynasty?" Kayla asked.

"I thought she was on the site?!" Kaitlyn spat at Taylor.

"She is, she just forgot about that part" Taylor defended.

Taylor logged onto Crave.com, a site for older men looking for younger women to go on dates with in return for cash. They took exclusive vacations, dinners, parties, or just spent time with the women. A Dynasty was an extremely wealthy guy who was verified by the site to have the confirmed means for the exotic lifestyle. Kayla was not willing before, but peer pressure set in, so she joined the site. She took $300 from her brother's piggy bank to buy a gift to sign up.

Most women who signed up don't have to be financially stable they just needed to be pretty. At 5'9 122 lb., brown hair, hazel eyes, a pearly white smile, and a 32-24-34 figure at 18, Kayla Vaughn was just that. They had bottles of Beautiful Moscato which became a popular brand amongst the millennials and other celebrities. The group of girls toasted to Kayla's birthday and talked about some experiences they had from the site. Kaitlyn told Kayla that her guy had a friend that Kayla should meet. Kayla had already been talking to a guy, but she wouldn't meet up with the guy until she was of age.

When they arrived at Pure, they were in complete awe of the famed lounge. So many of their celebrity idols were on the red carpet and going inside. Kayla could barely contain herself as they were escorted to a VIP section. To the far left of the lounge an area was surrounded by red sheer curtains. The area seated 14 people and it was catered with a bartender. The girls were taking selfie after selfie and posting it to their Tuvuler accounts.

When the men arrived, Kayla was absolutely stunned. Her whole body grew cold and she wanted to hide. She couldn't believe who she saw, nor did Ed Royal. When Kayla saw Royal kiss Kaitlyn everything came together. She immediately knew where Kaitlyn received all of her money and gifts. To make matters worse he literally sat next to Kayla.

The men were much older than she imagined; not like the guy she was chatting with online. The guy she was chatting with was probably the same age as her mom if not slightly younger. These guys are old enough to be her grandfather. Kaitlyn was paired with Ed Royal the attorney, Taylor was with John Carter, Ed's accountant, Stephanie was with Mitzer Donavich a German businessman, Mecca was by herself, for her guy was allegedly with the club, and Kayla was paired with Antonio Bordeliano, an Italian wine owner who was also an art enthusiast.

Everything was going fine as all the men were basically talking with each other as the girls talked amongst themselves. They would frequently engage each other then go back to their real interests. Friendly contact was made occasionally with kisses on the cheek, yet Kayla noticed how Ed Royal continued to look at her, and so did Kaitlyn. Ed Royal seemed to make it a point to continue to brush Kayla in certain way. Like on the arm when reaching for something or placing his knees to hers. She could see Kaitlyn growing a bit irritated, so Kayla wanted to go to the restroom. When they got into the restroom to freshen up Kayla told Kaitlyn what she knew.

"Kaitlyn, how long have you known your guy?"

"For a while I suppose. He isn't the worst, but he does treat me well. Why do you ask?" Kailyn was applying her lip gloss in the mirror.

"Because I know him." All the girls looked at her.

"Really?" Taylor asked. "How?" Stephanie asked.

"My mom works for him and his law firm," Kayla said.

"Bitch!" Mecca said.

"This is so weird," Taylor said.

"Well, what are you worried about? It's not like he said anything" Kaitlyn said.

"I know but it's just...you know...weird." Kayla said fidgeting.

"You don't have to worry about it, believe me, he has his hands full already and tonight will be no different," she said pulling her dress up at her breast.

"You mean you and him have...you know" Kayla alleged.

"Sure, lots of times and he isn't like the boys from school he is romantic about it."

"How was it?" Taylor asked.

"It's actually better. You can tell a man from a boy" she looked persuasively.

"Eww gross" Kayla spat. Kaitlyn almost jumped down her throat.

"Don't act all high and mighty like you're better than us."

"That's not what I meant" Kayla protested.

"Well, what did you mean?" Mecca asked with the rest of the girls staring at Kayla.

"It's...I mean" Kayla's eyes darted around as to look for the right thing to say.

"She's a virgin" Taylor interrupted. "Give the girl a break." Kayla was embarrassed. Kaitlyn, Stephanie, and Mecca laughed.

"Well, that explains it," Stephanie said mockingly. "Doesn't she know these guys like experience? They want a woman, not a kid." The girls continued laughing at Kayla.

"Guess we'll have to take your guy too," Mecca said sharply.

They turned to walk out, and she heard Stephanie ask Kaitlyn, "Did she even have her period yet or is she waiting on that too?" They continued laughing at her while walking out the door.

Kayla's feelings were hurt. She wanted to leave at that very instant, but Taylor told her that she shouldn't worry because Kaitlyn was just mad that she was prettier, and she thinks Ed likes her. If Ed leaves her she has nothing, and she overheard him say she was spending too much money. Even though this didn't completely cheer her up it was a step in the right direction. She battled with being a virgin for a long time.

She and Jason even made out on one occasion when they dated. It was only when it got too heated and she didn't want to do it that he started to date Kaitlyn. Things will change soon enough she told herself as she had every plan to lose her virginity. That's what she discussed with the guy on the website. He wanted to sleep with a virgin and in turn, he would give her 10K. She could use that money plus what her mom gave her along with a loan to pay for her college education. Yes, her plan was going to work, and she would not have to worry about anything else anymore.

They left the bathroom and went back to their section. Kaitlyn was between Antonio and Ed. Taylor looked at Kayla then grabbed her by the hand. Dean and Anderson Paak's song "Put my hands on you" started to play as if it were in a queue. When the song started Taylor danced with Kayla. Taylor was just the blonde version of Kayla standing at 5'9 32-24-36. All the men in

234

their section immediately focused their attention on the two girls.

It was as if they were moving in slow motion with their bodies in unison. Kailyn was jealous, so she tried to distract Ed by whispering in his ear. His eyes were still locked on Kayla, so she grabbed Mecca and Stephanie. It looked like the sexiest dance-off ever in that section with both groups trying to out-dance each other. Ed Royal, being the most adventurous out of the men got up and stood between the girls.

"Now this is the life boys, aye?!" he chuckled.

His hand slipped down the backs of Kayla and Stephanie. They dropped to their lower backs and went further down. Kayla was uncomfortable as she felt Mr. Royal's hand around her backside. She continued to dance but inside she was crying. She felt dirty...she felt ashamed.

Later that morning after Taylor and Kayla got back to Kayla's house, Taylor fell asleep when Kayla opened her Crave.com account. She had 26 new messages...most from her chatting with bmw750g. He was easy to talk to and Kayla found him to be very attractive. She actually looked forward to talking to him as he made her feel like an adult when they talked. He didn't treat her as if she was a child. They talked about worldly things and she taught him about some things as well.

She grew fond of him despite his interest which he never pressured her about it, unlike some other guys that made it obvious they just wanted sex. She was responding when she saw a message more recent buy a member tagged 'RoyalTreatment'. The subject was "I know you." She immediately got nervous, and wanted to delete the message, but was curious. What she read made her sick to her stomach. She started to cry and wished she never got on the site.

That morning after breakfast she told Taylor about the message. To her surprise, Taylor thought it was completely harmless. She told Kayla that she just needed to talk to him, set her boundaries, then at that point she would have nothing to worry about. After considering Taylor's input, she thought it over again and realized Taylor was right. The message simply stated that he wanted her and that he would do whatever he needed to do to have her. She contemplated a response and would get back to him later. Right now, she had her sights on her own interests.

Kayla and BMW750G were going to chat live on the site for the third time to discuss the arrangement of their date and expectation. One thing Kayla knew was that she had to have a Plan B pill and a condom, so she would not get pregnant. Her mom would be gone with Brady, so she would have the house all to herself. She would wear something provocative to turn him on. They were scheduled for 3 p.m. that day and she promised Taylor all the juicy details. She placed light makeup on with some lip gloss to keep a natural look as BMW750G didn't like a bunch of makeup.

This was fine by her because Kayla didn't really need much anyway. She looked in her top drawer and removed black sheer underwear and a black sheer bra. She fluffed her hair to give it a little more volume even though it was straight. It was just 5 minutes till when Tate chimed into her Tuvuler to chat. Tate was one of her original friends she made when she moved there. He wasn't popular, but he was okay with all the groups at school. The girls pretty much took over her social life and she distant from Tate. He still checked in on her because he was a genuine friend.

He had a thing for her but when he got the nerve to tell her she started to date, Jason. She put on her housecoat because she didn't want him to see her in such a revealing way.

"Hey Tate, what's up?"

"Hey K! I wasn't even sure you were going to pick up."

"Oh yeah? I'm here just getting situated before I head out."

"Oh, okay well I don't want to disturb you then. I can get with you later."

"No, I have a few minutes. What's up?" she said not trying to be rude.

"Well, I wanted to wish you a Happy Birthday since I didn't get an invite to the gathering you had last night."

She immediately felt embarrassed. How could she not have invited him? He was the only person who had been genuinely nice to her.

"Oh my God. Tate, I'm so sorry. Things have been so crazy with my mom I just wasn't thinking straight."

"No apologies I completely understand."

"I'm really sorry Tate."

"Please don't be Kay it's really all right."

"Hey how about I make it up to you. What are you doing on Saturday? We could hang out then?"

"Saturday I'm supposed to hang out with my uncle, but it will not be in until late so sure."

"Okay great then I will get back with you that morning and we can meet up at the mall okay?"

"Okay cool," he said. "Well Happy belated Birthday."

"Thank you so much and I'm sorry about the party, but I'm looking forward to Saturday," she said. "Okay talk to you later."

"Okay bye," he said.

When she changed screens, she had two missed calls on her Crave.com account messenger. She took off her housecoat revealing her breasts but decided she will leave it on and get him to ask her to take it off. She wanted to show him she could take directions and offer him a show. Her messenger started to chime again, and it was him.

"Hello, handsome."

"Hello there, how are you?"

"I'm good thanks for asking just getting situated."

"Oh yeah?"

"Yep. Had a night out with my girlfriends last night."

"That's right yesterday was your birthday wasn't it?"

"Yes, it was," she said as if he didn't know.

"I got you something he said."

"You did? What is it?"

"Open the door and you'll find out," he said.

"Huh?" she asked, and at that very moment the doorbell rang.

She was immediately scared looking at him on the video seeing him in his office.

"Don't worry it isn't me," he said noticing her concern.

She left her computer to check the door. When she opened it, it was a UPS delivery guy.

"Afternoon ma'am. I have a delivery for Ms. Kayla Vaughn."

"That's me. I'm Kayla."

"Sign here please" he handed her an electronic clipboard.

She signed in the box for her name and a receipt printed off where he gave her the pink copy. He handed her three boxes. One was long, the second one was about half the size of the first one, and the third was small.

"Thank you," she said.

"Have a nice day ma'am." He turned and left.

She shut the door, placed the receipt on top of the boxes then took them back upstairs. BMW750G was still on the video but he was on the phone. She looked at him with a smile.

She mouthed, 'How did you know where I stayed?' He looked down and wrote on a pad. He held the pad up after he finished writing and the message said he has superpowers that he got out of a Cracker Jacks box. She just looked at him. He wrote something else and held up the pad and it said, 'Googled picture hope you don't mind'. She sat back and thought. Of course! You can google a picture and it could show you if that picture had been used on the internet before.

The one he used for his search was of her at the Jersey Shore last summer in her bathing suit. It was also on her social media page. She nodded and said, 'It's okay.' He wrote something else and held it up and it said, 'if it's too weird we can call it off and you can keep the gifts no hard feelings.' She mouthed 'No is fine.' He nodded and gave her a thumb up. She shook the box. He pointed to the phone and made a hand puppet opening and closing it as he crossed his eyes. She laughed out loud.

He pointed at her then pulled at his shirt. She mouthed 'You like?' He nodded. She mouthed 'You want to see more?' He nodded. She stood. He wrote something down. When she looked closer the note said 'Slowly.' She winked at him. She backed up, so he could see her

241

from the thighs up. She slowly took the housecoat off while doing a little dance. She turned around allowing it to hang on her arms to her lower back then allowed it to slide down her ass.

When she turned around he had his fist in his mouth. She mouthed 'You like?' while rubbing her stomach and breasts. He nodded. He pointed to the presents and told her to open them. She took the long one, removing the red ribbon and inside was 18 long stem roses with a card that read Happy Birthday. She smelled them and smiled at him mouthing 'Thank you.' He nodded saying sure thing to whoever was on the phone with him and hung up.

"Sorry about that he said."

"No problem I understand you have to work and I know you must allow a man to be a man, so if a man needs to work a woman should be his support and not his stress."

"Wow you are amazing you know that?"

She smirked and opened the second box and it was a pair of 8 1/2 Noble Society heels with diamonds in them.

"Oh...my...God" she was shocked. "These haven't even come out yet how did you manage to..."

"Hey, I know people and you deserve it. You have been very respectable about all of this and I wanted to do something special for you."

She was teary-eyed. The shoes were supposed to be around $2,000 and no one had them. She ran her fingers over the beautiful emblem that was a custom design.

"Wow, I don't know what to say."

"Don't say anything. I just want you to be happy" he said.

"I am...I mean now I really am" she said with tears in her eyes.

"Well, in that case, you're really going to love the last box."

"Really?"

"Yes."

She opened it and reality hit her. She started to cry looking at him.

"I wanted you to have it regardless if you changed your mind. You have been a breath of fresh air for me even though we had an agreement. I think just being able to talk to you and getting to know you was enough" he said. She just looked at him.

"Do you mean that?" she asked.

"Yes, I do. We could walk away from each other right now and I would still be grateful to just have met such an amazing woman."

She was crying and wiped her tears. "Say the word and we could call this whole thing off." he said. She looked at the money in her hand and then looked at him.

ASTORIA QUEENS

"**K**ayla can you bring your laundry down?!...
Kayla!...Kayla!"

"She left mom."

"What? Where did she go?"

"The mall I guess. She said she was going to meet her friend."

"Why didn't she tell me?"

"She did. She said Mooomm I'm going to the mall with my friiieeends" Brady screamed out loud.

'Lord', Sheila thought to herself. She went upstairs to Kayla's room and clothes were all over the place. 'Teenagers' she thought. She started picking up clothes and putting them in the basket. She straightened her bed and fluffed her pillows. She went into the bathroom and picked up a good amount of clothes off the floor. She picked up a red dress, held it up, and looked at the name 'Louis Vuitton'. 'Jesus', she said to herself thinking if she was 20 pounds lighter and 20 years younger she would be a knockout in that dress. Huh! Glory years. She saw the roses from the mirror behind her. She put the dress in the basket then walked back into Kayla's room.

245

She set the basket on the bed then went to the dresser that the flowers sat on. She stopped to smell the flowers for a second and almost envied how romantic Dan used to be with her. She sat on the bed looking around as her baby was about to leave for college soon. It had been a long road raising her and Brady, but she did the best she could with what she had. Kayla was smart and was extremely well behaved. Never been in trouble, her grades were good, and she had some good friends. Her baby was going to be all right.

Sheila took a deep breath as she looked at the photo box on Kayla's nightstand and she picked it up to have a proper view. It was a cube of photos with her and her friends, but also of Kayla, Sheila and Brady. Kayla was a great kid and she was loved regardless of how her dad walked out on them. She placed the cube back on the desk, but she noticed a pink slip under it. It was a receipt that had to be signed for. When Sheila saw the sender, her heart fell to her stomach. She dropped the cube, it opened and a stack of hundred-dollar bills fell out. She turned white as she picked up the money as her mind raced. "Oh my God" she said. "Oh my God, Kayla!" she ran out of the room to get her phone.

Sheila called Kayla 6 times, but she didn't answer the phone. Sheila called Taylor, but Taylor said she hadn't spoken with her since earlier. She called Stephanie, but

Stephanie and Kaitlyn were at Mecca's and they hadn't spoken to her either. Sheila went to the mall but there was no sign of Kayla. When she returned home, Tate was at the door with a present in his hand.

"Hey Tate, how are you?"

"Hey, Ms. Vaughn. I'm fine, how are you?"

"A nervous wreck actually. Have you seen Kayla?"

"We were supposed to meet at the mall, but she never showed so I came by to drop off a present since I didn't get invited to the party."

Sheila knew Tate was a good friend to Kayla and he was good by her. How could Kayla not invite him to the party.

"What time were you two supposed to meet?"

"We were to meet at 3 because I was to go to my aunt and uncle's later for the weekend. I called her, but I just got voicemail."

"Where could she be?" Sheila asked rhetorically as she placed one hand on her hip and the other on her forehead trying not to draw too much worry.

"Have you called her other friends?"

"Yes, all of them and no one has seen her. That's not like her."

"I can look around if that will help. I just need to stop by my aunt and uncle's then I could check around" Tate offered.

"If it's not any trouble Tate."

"No trouble at all I will call when I'm on my way back or if I hear something."

"Okay thanks," Sheila said.

"Mom where's Kayla?" Brady sighed.

"I don't know son," Sheila said with tears in her eyes.

She reached in her purse and grabbed the pink slip and saw the name again. She was getting furious by the second then pulled out her cell phone. She looked through her contacts and found the number she was looking for. She pressed call.

TEXT

Babes your mom is out looking for

you. Where are you? Hmb -Taylor

EAST MANHATTAN

Tate pulled up to his aunt and uncle's home, a place he often visits to spend his weekends He really admired them and found them to be some of the most influential people in the city of New York. They had a solid relationship and both are successful in their industries. He tried to call Kayla again but still didn't get an answer.

"Hey Kayla, it's Tate...was just by your place dropping off your present when your mom showed. She is worried about you. Call home." he said on her voicemail.

TEXT

Call your mom -Tate

Tate got out of his 2008 C300 Mercedes and grabbed his bag out of the trunk. He didn't see his uncle's car, nor did he see his aunt's. He had a key, so he would just let himself in as he did on all other occasions. They both probably will be home sometime soon, so he would just make himself at home and into the fridge. When He opened the door, he set his bag down and headed to the kitchen. He opened the double doors and grabbed a soda. There were some Forbes, Rob Reports, Businessweek's, and Watch magazines on the counter.

He opened Forbes and skimmed an article of how Robert Louis had been in jail and why you should invest in his companies. He really liked his story just like most Americans. He grabbed some chips out of the butler's pantry, then went upstairs to the guest room. He was walking down the hall past his aunt and uncle's room and into the guest room. He was about to open the door when he backed up to his aunt and uncle's room. The door was cracked about an inch. He looked into the center of the room where the bed was. He couldn't take his eyes off her. It was Kayla and she was being fucked doggy-style by his uncle Brandon Matthews.

BROOKLYN BRIDGE

"There must be some mistake, Sheila," Kristen said. Brandon doesn't even know Kayla. Why would he send her flowers for her birthday and money?"

"I have a receipt from him as the sender from the UPS service. It has his name and company address on it. Where are you Kristen?" asked Sheila.

"I'm headed to the house. I will be there in 20 minutes."

"I'm about the same distance out so I will meet you there" Sheila said.

250

"Okay" Kristen responded.

EAST MANHATTAN

———

Tate went back downstairs stunned by what he just saw. He was sitting at the island in the kitchen when Brandon and Kayla came downstairs. Kayla turned ghostly white and was instantly silent. Brandon tried to speak but Tate interrupted.

"I saw you."

"It's not what you think," Brandon said.

"I saw you," Tate said again.

"Look your aunt and I..." Brandon tried to explain.

"We've been looking for you all day" Kayla just held her head down. "Your mom has been trying to reach you," he said.

"My mom Is dead Tate what are you talkin' about?" Brandon said. Tate looked at Kayla then Brandon finally got it.

"You two know each other?" Brandon asked.

"Tate I'm sorry," his uncle said. "Can we talk about this later I need to get her..." and before he finished Kristen and Sheila came in through the front door.

ASTORIA QUEENS 3 DAYS LATER

Tate sat in front of Kayla's home with the letter in his hand contemplating if he should give it to her. The past couple of days had been more than eventful, and a pain he had never felt before. Seeing his uncle have sex with Kayla was extremely hurtful to his soul. He couldn't believe it nor did it seem real. But the truth was in fact that it was. How could this be? Why did this have to happen? He tried his best and would have given Kayla anything. He thought to himself why is it the ones you love so much, hurt you so badly, and not want you? His uncle of all people in the world. How could he do this to him? He poured out his heart to Kayla in the note.

It revealed his true feelings for her and hoped she would realize how much he loved her. It was just an addition to him saying he had his uncle send the flowers and shoes for him to her for her birthday. He told them that Kayla had shown up at his uncle's trying to figure out who it was that sent the money and presents. He told them his uncle was explaining it all to Kayla when he arrived and she didn't answer her phone because she forgot to take it off silent. It was a reach, but he bailed them out. Kristen and Sheila bought it and called him a really great friend for wanting to take money from his account to help Kayla with her college tuition.

Sheila wanted him to take the money back, but he couldn't because it wasn't his to take back. He called her later that night trying to get her to explain, but his efforts were unsuccessful. So, he figured this letter would be his last attempt. He kissed the letter and told himself here goes nothing. He got out of the car and he paused to look at Kayla's room. Walking to the door he saw Brady's bike on the sidewalk, so he grabbed it and put it in the yard. A good kid he thought. He rang the doorbell and Sheila came to open it.

"Hey Tate, how are you?"

"I'm fine Ms. Vaughn is Kayla home?"

"Sure, come on in."

"No thanks, I will only be a second."

"Oh okay. Is everything all right?" she asked with slight concern.

"Oh yes sure I just left my car running and I just wanted to drop off this letter is all."

"Sure thing," she said. "I'll get her one second."

Sheila went to the bottom of the steps and called for Kayla.

"Kayla!" she yelled.

"Yes?!" she called from upstairs.

"You have company."

"Okay, she responded."

Sheila looked at Tate and walked to him touched him on the arm looking at the letter. "Good luck," she said to him with a warm smile.

He looked at her shyly and told her thanks. Sheila went back to the kitchen. Tater came running to the door with Brady right behind. Tate kneeled and patted the energetic pit-bull on the head.

"Hey Tater," he said with the dog wagging his tail.

"Hey, Tate. I got to take Tater for a walk. You wanna come?" Brady asked.

"Maybe next time kiddo."

"Okay come on Tater," he said as the dog pulled him out the door.

Kayla surfaced at the top of the stairs. She had on blue pajama pants with penguins on them, and a white fitted tank top. She came down the stairs and Tate took her in with every step. When she reached the bottom, she came to the door, moved some hair over her right ear, and crossed her arms across her stomach boosting her breasts. She looked at him with complete embarrassment.

"Hi," she said.

"Hey" he responded.

"What's up?"

He couldn't help but notice that even in pajamas and a tank top she was still so naturally gorgeous.

"I wasn't able to reach you, so I just came by to...to give you this." He held on to the letter. She looked at him not knowing what to say.

"I just want you to know that I'll always be here for you Kayla and I love you." She looked at him with tears starting to fill her eyes. She felt so horrible about all that happened and wished she could take it all back, but she couldn't. He handed her the letter and she took it with her right hand. Her left arm was still across her waist. She looked down at it then look back up at Tate. He smiled, then pulled a black .38 revolver out, put it in his mouth, and squeezed the trigger.

REASON 9

HE'S A CELEBRITY

Although there are many industries that have successful patrons there are none that I'm more familiar with than those in the music industry, so I will focus my explanation on this particular "famer" as they tend to associate with all the other famous people. For this particular reason, I'm not speaking from opinion, I'm speaking from actual experience. In my defense let me first say no I am not famous, nor have I been...well not directly anyway. Let me explain my position so you can get a clear understanding.

As far as I can remember I've always wanted to be in the music industry. I grew up around it as my father played gospel music for several groups and still does to this day. Though it was gospel music it still had many attractive perks. Food, money, and attention from many people especially women. I would notice how some group members would talk about how all the hot women in the churches would look at them. I was young, but I could put two and two together. Knowing my dad, I'm sure he had his fair share...actually, I'm certain of it. Attaboy pop! Sorry, Mom.

Any who! As time went on, I danced enough to Soul Train in my living room picking up dance moves, and I knew it was my calling...the music industry. I already was known as a great hip hop dancer from house parties, clubs, and high school talent shows. However it wasn't until about 2002 when I began to focus on being a rapper just like 30,000 other people. I was good...I mean really good. Some say I sounded like Mase and 50 Cent all in one which was cool with me because they were huge stars. I was promoting with my cousin TR who was an R&B artist working with Steve Mayfield at the time. We were also running with his label mate Cheetah Man who was performing shows with Little Scrappy and had a mega-hit out.

I was in a crew called K.P.N.C. and we were a local hit. So, you could tell I was around music a good bit. Since I was around music, it led to clubs, which meant I was around a lot of women. See being in a hot crew meant you had a good chance to succeed, and everyone wants to be down with you or around you and your crew...especially women. Nothing said women like R&B and being around TR meant plenty of them. I remember this one chick named "Jennifer" who wanted to be a dancer. We hit it off instantly and she told me she knew me from seeing me at some shows. I had her at my place that very same night. She said she wanted to be our backup dancer. She never became our dancer, but she did work on some music with me.

Another was "Elle" who I met at a club who wanted to get next to Pastor Troy so bad that she gave me fellatio in the parking lot. "Jess" slept with me the same night we did a show in KP with RnR. As time and shows went on with some of the biggest names in music from 50 Cent, Mobb Deep, Yang Yang Twins, Lil Jon, Snoop Dogg, R Kelly, Lil Wayne, Usher, Goodie Mob, etc., all added to my list of erotic experiences with women. How? Because I was the opening act or promoter. Mostly the promoter. Women would throw themselves at me simply because it could get them closer to the celebrity.

Famous people attract the most beautiful and boldest individuals that you could ever imagine. Take Brad Pitt, George Clooney, Eminem, Hugh Grant, Shamar Moore, etc for example. These guys are rock stars of the world and have millions literally millions of women and men that just want to be attached to them because success is the most addictive drug on the planet. Success breeds the cream of the crop and could solve all types of issues. Commit a crime and no one knows you, you're going to jail. Commit a crime while being famous, being famous will get you out of it. Get caught cheating on your wife when you're famous and it's swept under the rug. Try that while not being famous, and the husband is left quicker than a climax out of a guy fresh off a ten-year bid.

Nowadays with social media, the ability to become famous in an instant is greater than your chances of the Carolina Panthers winning the Super Bowl. With Twitter, Snapchat, Facebook, Instagram, and Tuvuler, the more followers you have, the more you are a form of celebrity. Even corporate giants become supporters by paying social media "Influencers" to advertise on their page.

So, what does that mean for someone who has no real ambition or drive to achieve the maximum out of life? It means the very second you act as if you can't be replaced someone else is taking your position. A lot of women get caught up in the Beyoncé empowerment songs but forget they are not Beyoncé. I'm a big fan of Beyoncé and her music. Please do not misinterpret my statement, yet you need to love yourself like that song by Mary J Blige says and you most certainly will if you are with someone famous because the bold do not care about you.

You know all those model type women that be at the NBA and NFL games looking at the LeBrons, Peppers, Jacksons, Newtons and the Currys in professional sports? They are dying to get those guys and when they do they make it really easy for those guys not worrying about getting to know them. They are content knowing when the famous calls, it will be an A list reward for them, as well as the famous guy.

So, if you happened to be with someone that is a celebrity or famous I'm sure you have had that feeling already. All I can say is if you sweep your emotions under the rug make sure you go back and put it in the trash before you go crazy. As soon as you go crazy, the famous celebrity will remain famous, and you, my dear will go to jail. To the left to the left...you better love yourself.

SEE WHAT HAD HAPPENED WAS

Robert Louis was still sitting in his sponsored section at Fite's Cigar Bar when his waitress brought him his third shot of Victor O'Neill cognac. He was halfway through his Cuban cigar yet still at the beginning of his dilemma. What in God's name was going on with his life? He thought sure, on the surface, he was on top of the world. However there was a lot that still was not adding up. His companies were in the black, his personal life...well it was kind of black.

Sooner or later he would need to come to terms with his past relationships and understand they were just learning experiences. Yet 42 years of the learning experiences was enough. He wanted to settle down and just come home to a family. Why did love have to be so damn difficult? Why couldn't it just be two people agreeing to not screw each other over and make a great life with a successful family? What the hell makes a woman truly happy? The thought alone made him down his whole shot.

"You drink too much of that shit, and you're going to need assistance getting out the door. I thought you quit anyway."

"I did."

"So, what happened?"

"Went to an AA meeting the first night and ended up screwing my sponsor."

"Wow!"

"Yeah, I know. Very next day I wanted to start my own spirit line. Figured if quitting got me that lucky imagine what the hell owning the shit would do."

Robert and Fite both roared in laughter.

"How are you, Fite?"

"I'm good brother how about yourself?"

"Good, good. Sitting here figuring out where the hell my life is going."

"From the looks of it and the news seems like you're going straight to the bank" Fite laughed.

"Yeah I guess so, but damn that is all."

"What do you mean?"

"I mean is that it? Just going to the bank?"

"Am I speaking to the same person that would come out of his cell with a pencil and paper in his hands every day for almost two years talking about nothing but business? The same guy that had more ambition in his finger than people had in their bodies?"

"Now you're just being funny," Robert said.

"Hell, if I am man! People see you and get a really good vision of what rags-to-riches, being focused, and having complete faith is. What being committed can really do for you if you truly want something. I know personally what I see in you" he paused looking around his lounge. "I mean when I walk in this place, I don't just see my lounge I see your friendship and brotherhood." Robert looked at his friend. "Man, you remember how it was for me in jail before I met you?" Fite said. "I had no family support and I was barely even eating. I had so-called family that just abandoned me. My brother had my car but wouldn't even send me $20 for me to get something from the commissary. My own flesh and blood. Then you, a complete stranger gave me a $0.85 soup."

"I'm still mad as hell Mecklenburg County Jail charged inmates $0.85 for a damn soup when you can get 10 for a dollar," Robert said. They both laughed.

"Yeah but that soup got me through," Fite said.

"Yeah them soups got us through a lot of hard times" Robert agreed.

"Well if you are having that hard of a time, I can go make you a swole right now. You know I'm mean with hot water and a bag."

"Oh, hell no! I don't want another noodle for as long as I live" they laughed.

"But seriously Rob all jokes aside had it not been for you and your insane dedication this lounge wouldn't exist nor would CF and I'm grateful. If I could do anything you know it's yours."

"I'm a good man just a little woe is me when I've had a few that's all."

"You sure?"

"Yeah, brother I'm good. Thank you."

Robert knew Fite was genuine and sincere. They went through a lot when they were locked up and since then they became brothers as well as good business partners with the hottest venues in the southeast.

"So, what are you up to anyway?"

"Yeah, that's why I came over. Someone is here for you. Said she was supposed to meet you here."

"Oh yeah, Jenna told me I should meet this lady. Told me it would change my life."

"What? Is she a psychic or something?" Fite asked.

265

"I don't know but she made it sound important though."

"Oh okay. Well, I will send her over and if you need anything let me know" Fite stood extending his hand to Robert.

"Okay I will," Robert said shaking his hand.

Fite started to walk off then he turned.

"Hot one she is?"

"Who?" Robert asked.

"The lady that's here to see you."

"Who is she?"

"I don't know but she ain't from here though."

"Why do you say that?"

"Accent" Fite said and he walked off.

Robert sat and wondered who on earth it could be. Jenna was extremely vague when she told him about his visitor. He kicked himself for not getting more info about her as he was one for being well informed. There would be no need to wait any longer because the mysterious woman was making her way to his table. She was about 5'8, 140 lbs, light caramel skin, jet black long hair, olive-shaped eyes, in her late 30s early 40s, and Spanish. She wore long black slacks with a black wedge heel. Her red blouse was loose fitting and she wore a small gold necklace with a cross. She was gorgeous he thought as he stood.

'Buenas Noches senior Robert. It has been a long time no?'

"Buenas Noches, Como Esta's senorita?"

"Vergara," she said. "English is ok we speak yes?"

"Yes, yes, of course, please have a seat." He pulled out the large red velvet chair for her. She smiled saying thank you.

"Would you care for something to drink Ms. Vegara?"

"Jess I will havt what chor havting." Her thick accent was quite obvious

The waitress immediately poured a shot of Victor O'Neill.

"You must excuse me Ms. Vegara I was not prepared for this meeting as my attorney gave me little to no detail about you. Please excuse me if I am misdirected." She sat eyeing him with a smile on her face admiring him and said nothing.

"Ms. Vegara, you mentioned it has been a long time. Have we met before?" he asked.

She continued to smile then said, "Jess we havt."

"Okay, can you recall where? Perhaps a business meeting or convention of sorts?"

"No," she said now looking around the lounge as if she was out of place.

She took a small sip of the shot to taste, looked as if it was okay and then took the whole shot. Robert just looked at her.

"May I havt anoter please?" she asked. The waitress poured her another then stepped back to the side. She then took the whole shot and looked at Robert.

"Ms. Vegara I'm sorry but..."

"It was on TV."

"Excuse me? What was on TV?"

"Chor life was on TV and I see."

"You saw me on TV that's where you know me from?"

"No," she said.

"I'm sorry I don't follow."

"I see you on TV, so I come and find you."

Robert immediately thought he knew what was going on. He had these kinds of experiences before now that he has made a good amount of money. Women coming out of nowhere saying they are in love with him in hopes of a secure financial future.

He was all too familiar in the move nor was he interested. He would not be disrespectful to her though as he was a gentleman. He thought why Jenna would have him meet her. Was it for charity? That's it. It was for charity. He was a major donator and always has been. He donated millions to MS research, muscular dystrophy, and to the Jeff Gordon Children's Hospital in Charlotte North Carolina. Jenna must have known it would be something he would donate to, to go through all of this.

"It has been years since I've seen you. I tried all I could for years to make sure I could reach you in case something happened. Life hasn't been bad for me. It has been goodt to me. I even got married but Fernando passed away."

Robert was completely blown away and lost as to what this woman was talking about. Who was she?

"I have not been with anyone since Fernando and we havt a wonderful family. All kids healthy. Fernando was and hast always been goodt to la nina but one day Fernando got sick and he talked out of his headt and that's when la nina got upset. I tried to do all I could to keep chor life chor life, but I did not do goodt and now all is a mess."

269

"What is a mess Ms. Vegara? Robert asked.

She reached in her purse and pulled out a picture of her, a man, two boys, and a girl then handed it to Robert. He was holding the picture when she pointed to the tall looking skinny girl.

"You have a beautiful family Ms. Vegara."

"I read chu never hadt more children and I think so did my la nina." She pointed at the girl that was super skinny.

"Anymore? What do you mean I don't have any children Ms. Vegara?" She looked stunned and taken back by his comment.

She then pulled out an older picture of her and the same girl, but the girl had long hair just the two standing in front of an old Honda.

"Ms. Vegara I'm sorry but..." she pulled out another picture. This time the picture was of Korina.

PURE LOUNGE

When Robert pulled up at his lounge with Ms. Vergara the lounge was busy as it normally was, so he decided to take the back entrance. Calling his brother Michael ahead of time, he asked him to get a hold of Korina. This one time the normally cool-headed owner was out of character as well as at a loss of words. When he got into his office his brother came to see what was going on and to know who the mysterious woman was he had with him. When Michael opened the door his eyes opened wide.

"Oh shit!" he said surprised. Ms. Vegara looked at Michael and smiled.

"Ah Senor Michael. It hast been a long time. How are chu?"

"Hola Senorita, Como Estas? Ha sido un largo tiempo."

"Bien Bien senor Lynn English please."

Robert stopped dead in his tracks from pacing the room behind his desk. He looked at the two confused.

"How do you know Ms. Vegara?" he asked.

"Ms. Vegara?" Michael asked.

"Yes," Robert confirmed.

"So, you did marry Fernando?" Michael asked spirited.

"Yes. We married for 19 years."

"Wait you know Ms. Vegara?" Robert asked his brother. Michael looked at Robert as if he was being disrespectful.

"Fat it's Amelia."

"Amelia? Amelia who?"

"My married name is Vegara but my maiden name is..."

Robert finished "Herrera" now remembering the summer of 2001 shocked sitting down slowly.

"Yes" she said smiling now that he remembered.

Looking at Michael, "How did you know?"

Michael went to the bar and made himself a nice healthy shot of Winecoff vodka. He held his glass up to Amelia and Robert, but they declined. He walked back over to sit beside Amelia at Roberts's desk.

"When you got indicted awaiting trial in the county I was checking on things at the house as usual. Well, one day I go by and your lovely ex-wife Meghana is all hysterical and shit. I get her calm and she tells me how this girl contacted her saying she was looking for you because

272

she was your daughter. She said her ill father told her that she was not his real daughter but his stepdaughter. She asked me did I know anything, and I told her I didn't."

"But you did I assume."

"Yes, I knew for years but Amelia thought it better you not know because her family would disown her. Mainly because you are not Hispanic and even more she had a one-night stand. I sent money on your behalf, but she never kept it."

Robert looked at Amelia. "Why?"

"Chor life was chor your life," she said somber and prideful standing on her value.

"Anyway, some time passed, and I got this wild call while checking on other matters. This woman or girl saying she was a reporter tells me she was doing a story and wanted to know if you had children that would be affected by the charges. I thought nothing until Meghana bought it up. With the people at her job looking at her funny, the indictment, and the allegation. Meghana couldn't take it and that's when she filed for divorce. Guess she figured you lied to her about wanting children all those years."

Robert's expression was as if he was reliving the pain of being abandoned by his wife all over again. He remembered how many nights he sat in his cell crying because he couldn't do anything about it. She knew he was not responsible for what happened, yet she turned cold towards him. He wrote letter after letter pleading for her not to give up on him, but she treated him like he was scum. It was because of that he vowed to focus on making great changes in his life that would always keep him in the heart of those who would appreciate him. At first, he thought it was a story she made up because she was having an affair with her brother's friend from college.

"When the lady called me again I traced the number and it was from Amelia's house. Amelia told me it was under control but apparently, your daughter was just as anxious to meet her father."

"So, you knew Korina was my daughter?"

"Yes, I got her DNA and had some tests ran."

"And just when the fuck was your plan to tell me that shit? Did you gotdamn consider the fact that I could have slept with my own gotdamn daughter?"

"Thought crossed my mind but you gave no explanation that you had, so I figured you hadn't. Plus think about it.

274

She knew she was your daughter so how fucked up would that be if she knowingly slept with you?"

"Korina has search chu for so long nothing would have stopped her until she got to the bottom of it all. She always knew she was different. So, when she was told she was chors she was seeing she could havt a better life. A better life than what me and Fernando could provide for her" Amelia said.

"All of this is so sudden and what am I supposed to do now? The media will have a damn field day with this shit."

"I say we embrace it" Michael suggested.

"You do?"

"Sure! The media will say what it looks like, but you can let them know you're just a father who wanted to handle things as a family. It will be hard for them to play it off as a relationship and it will be a bigger story knowing you got set on knowing your daughter instead of keeping it a secret. Matter of fact I think we should leak the story ourselves first so we can get ahead of it."

"What about Amelia? She will definitely get some slack for all of this."

"What is this slack you speak of? I'm not know of the meaning" she asked.

"Means the media will be in your life and may cause life to be a living hell for you and your family. They will talk negative about you and say other nasty things."

"I see. I've always known when Korina find out she would be mad but only her no one else" Amelia said.

"Yes, people nowadays are very cynical and self-centered and live through other people's lives. They do this because their own lives are shit" Michael said.

"So, what do we do now?" Robert asked.

"We get Korina and we get a press release out about what we know. I can get in touch with Mojo and she will know how to handle it all. Don't worry this will all be taken care of. One thing we know is that we can count or Korina to really blow this up and take every advantage of the opportunity" Michael said.

All they had to do now was find Korina. That night Mr. Louis had DJ Alex Guesta from Milan Italy to perform for an exclusive EDM set. He got in touch with Korina, Robert placed her, a couple of business associates, and Amelia in the front row section by the DJ booth. He almost walked them all down before Bishop told him his brother was talking with a detective and an FBI agent with some new associates of his. Some new associates Mr. Louis did not agree with.

Michael met these guys trying to launch a career of a rapper named Sunny Brixx who was NGA affiliated. Mr. Louis wanted to move forward with the venture, but the men came back with horrible records including investigations regarding the killing of an FBI agent. It also didn't help that Domingo was still at large and was associated with this group. Mr. Louis knew his brother would always have his best interest. He knew Michael would die for him, but Michael also could be extremely dangerous. He needed Michael and his group to relocate so he went down to get them out of this section and into another as tonight was for a bit of celebration.

"Sure, please confirm with my assistant and she will have everyone at the ready. Now if you would excuse me I need to shake my proverbial cup at Ms. Patton" Mr. Louis said to the detective and the FBI agent. As he walked off he couldn't help but feel odd about all that happened between the officers, his brother, and his brother's guests. It was a bit tense when he approached so he would need to find out more. He always did. He walked over to say hello to Candice Patton to tell her she was doing an amazing job on The Flash with hopes of working on a project he had an idea for.

He also said hello to a host of other phenomenal people in attendance like Full Frontal's Jenna Bee, artist Anicka Yi, model Cara Delevigne, This Time Tomorrow creator

Krystal Bick, beautiful actress Chrissie Fit, actress Priyanka Chopra, and artist Janelle Monae. He made a note to do a benefit concert with her as the headliner. Camila Cabello, Tony Dovocani, dancer Bryan Tanaka, Jordy Craig, Idris Elba, Beth Stern, Victoria Justice, hmmm what was she doing with Ben Affleck he thought. Nick Jonas, Sam Heughan who was doing well on Outlander, country music star Hunter Hayes, Bill Skarsgard, Ifenesh Haders, and many others as it was a routine of his to meet as many people as he could.

Always believing in the motto – your network determines your net worth. He made his rounds as usual then went to the dressing room of Alex to thank his longtime friend for coming and agreeing on such short notice. He worked with Alex on numerous occasions and all ended successfully. When he got back to his office Amelia, Korina, and others were all set for the performance. He figured they would get a chance to iron out everything tomorrow after the detective and agent questioned the staff about Domingo.

THE WARDOLF ASTORIA HOTEL

Robert was dropping off Amelia when the memory of how they met rekindled familiar emotions. He went up to her room and knocked on the door. She opened it and smiled when she saw it was him. Inviting him in, there he remained for the rest of the day.

CHANNEL 11 FOX NEWS NEW YORK BREAKING STORY

"Good morning. I'm Tonya Rogers with Channel 11 News with a report. Authorities have discovered what seems to be a heinous homicide of a federal agent who was investigating the death of actress Kimberly Reynolds. It was only weeks ago the actress was working on the blockbuster "The Queen" when she was suddenly taken off as the lead role and replaced with Korina Rodriguez. The Indigo hotel staff discovered Reynold's body in her hotel bathroom, and reported an unidentified male leaving the establishment. Special Agent Lindsay DuBaun was assigned to assist with the local 79th Precinct in Brooklyn headed by Detective Nick Morales. We are going live at the scene now with Gabrielle Jollie."

"Yes, Tonya what normally would be a quiet parking garage for residents at this apartment complex has turned into what authorities are saying to be the scene of the worst homicide this city has ever seen."

FAR ROCKAWAY NEW YORK

Ring! Ring! Ring! Ring!

"Nick!"

Ring! Ring!

"Nick!"

"Hmm?"

"Your phone is ringing."

"Okay!"

Morales looked up at the clock reading 3:27 a.m. He reached for his phone and answered.

"Hello?"

"Morales! It's Captain Fitzgerald."

"Yeah Captain. What is it?" he said wiping his eyes.

"Morales it's DuBaun."

Nick became instantly alert sitting up as the Captains tone was that of immediate attention for the worst.

"Captain what's going on? Where is DuBaun?"

"Nick you better get down here. Those animals"

Nick's heart sank into his stomach. He already knew by the Captain's tone...he just waited for him to deliver the blow. He just had an amazing night with Agent DuBaun and he felt they had a greater connection than before. Now he felt he never would see her again.

"Where Captain?"

"Her parking deck."

"I'll be there as soon as I can" and he hung up.

SOHO NEW YORK

Morales's Crown Vic came to a screeching stop as it pulled up in front of Michael Lynn's brownstone. He was accompanied by James Truth, Carmine Giovanni, Zayn Presley of the FBI, and Captain Fitzgerald among 12 other units.

"Wait!" Captain Fitzgerald said when Morales jumped out of the car. There was no listening. The FBI agents were getting out of their cars as Morales approached the door. He banged on the door as the agents and other officers were coming up his rear.

Bang! Bang! Bang! A light came on.

Bang! Bang! Bang!

"Hold on!" a voice said from inside the door.

Bang! Bang! "Open up! Police!"

Michael Lynn opened the door and Morales's fist crashed into his face. Michael hadn't had a chance to take a step back before Morales sent another brutal left hook into his chest. When Michael hit the ground, his jaw was already out of place. Morales looked to do the same with his ribs as he threw his weight into his right leg, breaking it into two.

"You son of a bitch!" Morales spat angrily.

He kicked Michael again then lifted him to his feet to deliver a punishing right hand to his left eye sending him over an end table. At that time Truth and Presley, two huge African American agents grabbed Morales who looked as if he could go another 12 rounds. Michael was bleeding badly from the eye and his face was swollen. Agent Giovanni picked him up off the ground and sat him hard on the sofa.

"What the fuck man? What the hell is wrong with you?" he screamed at Morales.

"You son of a bitch! I know it was you. You bastard!" Morales shouted.

He broke loose and managed to land another right hand clean into Michael's nose. Blood gushed everywhere.

"That's enough Detective back off!" Captain said.

"The fuck are y'all doing in my shit?" Michael questioned, grabbing his face in extreme pain.

"Listen, you piece of dog shit. I don't have the time nor patience to fuck around with you right now. I also have no problem allowing my detective to finish you off. Right here and right now. I want to know where you went when you left the club?"

"Shit man I can't breathe" he cried. "I'm going to sue the shit out of you punk motherfuckahs. You broke my fucking nose."

"Answer!" Agent Giovanni commanded.

"I came the fuck right back here where else would I go?"

"Who saw you come here? Was anyone with you?" Agent Truth said.

He pointed up the stairs, where two of the Asian women from the club were, half-naked holding each other scared. After quickly questioning the two Asian women, they confirmed they came back to the brownstone after leaving the club.

"Your two shithead friends, where are they?" Morales demanded.

"Man, I don't know and fuck you. You better have a damn good lawyer you piece of shit."

"Listen to me you dumb fuck a federal agent has been killed and if you don't tell me where your two little shit pals are you're going down with them."

"Bullshit you ain't putting nothing on me you fucking pig" he retorted.

"Where are they?" Agent Truth asked him, sternly grabbing his swollen face.

"Fuck! Fuck! Fuck! Aight! Aight! Man damn! Fort Greene projects apartment 12b 9th floor" he conceded.

Captain Franklin got on his radio and had dispatch route units to the address Michael just gave.

HAMPTONS NEW YORK

THREE WEEKS LATER

The winters in the Hamptons have a lower buzz of people compared to summers and springs. There is still a good amount of people who stick around. Many would be there for a weekend getaway, some to have romantic affairs, none of which called for Robert Louis to take time out of his hectic schedule, but definitely a valid reason. He arrived at the 5-bedroom 4.5 bathroom 8000 sq ft home just on the beach with bags of groceries from the market.

"Hello! Hello! Is anybody home?" he called.

"I'm upstairs. I'll be down in a minute" a female voice said.

"Okay. Take your time."

He went back out the door to retrieve more groceries. Having filled both arms he headed back into the house. He was placing them on the counter when she came down the stairs. She had on a long-sleeve white shirt with some grey sweatpants. Her hair was short, and the bandage was still around her head like an 8-inch headband from the last of her surgery. She walked into the kitchen and sat at the counter.

"Oh, there she is. How do you feel?"

"Better actually...especially when the meds kick in."

"I bet. How's your appetite?" he asked.

"Back with a vengeance. I swear I could eat a horse."

"I think that's against the law. I bought steak but if you want I know a guy."

"Eww no. Steak sounds amazing."

"Then steak and potatoes it is my dear, and while we eat I figured we can watch a classic."

He reached in a Target bag and produced a Blu-ray version of the movie "The Goonies."

"No way you found this" she grabbed it smiling.

"Yeah, I figured we could get a good laugh for old time sake," he said, still putting the groceries away.

"Definitely," she said holding the disc.

"No one said 'Aye you guys' like Kim," he said looking at the DVD. "I used to think Kim was Sloth," he said smiling.

"Stop it," she said.

"I did man she had it down packed."

"It was kind of creepy wasn't it," she said cringing.

"Hell yeah."

They both went quiet for a second then Robert felt he should let her know what he knew.

"Jenna," he said softly. She looked up at him with the thought of her best friend on her mind.

"Yes," she said looking back to him.

"They got him," he said looking into her eyes.

Jenna went silent for a moment.

"How? When? Tell me everything and leave out not one single detail" she said resettling in her chair giving Robert her undivided attention.

Robert looked at his friend and stopped putting away the groceries. He fixed themselves some vodka then he proceeded to explain how everything unfolded since the night she was shot by Justine and left in a coma.

3 WEEKS EARLIER

The authorities went to Fort Greene projects to apprehend Nation and LeTrais, but it led to a shootout leaving both of the men dead. Robert was with his brother to discuss what happened with his attorney when he got the message.

LAW OFFICES OR NICOLE LEWIS

"I want his ass arrested and thrown the fuck in jail right gotdamn now" Michael shouted.

"I'm afraid it's not that simple Mr. Lynn."

"How the fuck ain't it simple? Look at my fucking face!" Michael pointed.

"You are asking a bunch of cops and federal agents who just lost one of their own to a brutal attack to say you were assaulted by one of their own while you were buddy-buddy with the men that killed Special Agent DuBaun of the FBI."

"But they are the ones that killed those guys and I wasn't no fuckin' buddy-buddy with them either. I was just out for the deal with Sunny Bricks."

"Doesn't matter you, in their eyes, are part of that group, and until something bigger is presented you will always be on their shit list."

"So, this detective gets away with beating my ass and all I get is the doctor bill?"

"No, I'm not saying that Mr. Lynn.

"Well what the hell are you saying?" he grunted.

"Michael she is only trying to help" Robert chimed in.

"How is telling me I can't do shit helping?"

"Mr. Lynn you can file for assault, but two things are against you. One, the two witnesses you had were not legal US citizens. They can get deported and you can be in jail for human trafficking, a far more serious issue."

"How the hell was I to know them chicks weren't legal? Not something I normally ask on the first date" he said looking between his brother and the attorney.

"The second thing is that it's easy for them to say you were resisting arrest and with your criminal history the judge might just buy it. Judges always tend to side with law enforcement and with this case you can count on it."

"So, what are you saying?"

"I'm saying the best we will get is a statement of public suspension with pay pending an investigation which will drag out for years. Ultimately getting him off and giving the lounge negative publicity. I can see getting the medical covered but that's about it" she said.

"This is some absolute bullshit. What the fuck do we pay you for if all you're going to do is get the cops off?" he stood and stormed out the door.

292

Attorney Lewis continued with Robert when a text message came from his assistant.

You have a package at the office

...says urgent - Holly

Okay thanks -CEOR

Robert concluded the meeting with his attorney and met with his brother downstairs in front of the building smoking a cigarette.

"You didn't have to be so rude. You should apologize. She was only trying to help."

"I know, and I will. It's just fucked up how cops can get away with beating the shit out of people no matter who they are."

"Oh, trust me I know. I've seen my fair share of mistreatment by COs while in prison. They would treat us like animals and you couldn't do anything because they had ways of giving you the business or putting you in cells with guys who would" Robert said.

"They are all assholes if you ask me. Low-life cowards who were bitches in high school who became cops to feel empowered. Badge don't make them tough though. Shit, let you know they are pussy."

293

"That may be so but as long as they have it there is always the fight," Robert said.

"Yeah, where are you headed?" Michael asked, taking a drag from his Newport.

"Got to head back to the office got some business to handle."

"Need me to help?" Michael asked.

"Nah I'm good. I'll see you later tonight. Make sure you go apologize."

"Aight I will. Cool." he shook his brother's hand and got into the waiting black SUV. His brother walked back into the building.

CONDE NAST

The package was in a priority mail envelope, sealed, but had no return address. 'Urgent' was written on it with black marker. When Robert asked Holly, who brought it over she said a bike messenger said some guy gave him $100 to send it up so he did. When he opened it, it was a USB drive. He plugged it in his computer and the contents were nerve-rattling. It was images of all kinds of activity in his club. Drugs being sold by Domingo, Domingo coming out of the Indigo Hotel the day Kim was found dead, IDs of under aged girls pictured with prominent figures like Ed Royal, and the mayor. There were also images of Jenna and Kim in different places as if they were followed. His hands began to shake.

He saw a note that said 'Call this number now. I'm watching.' He looked around and wondered who the hell it was. He picked up his phone and called the number. It was answered on the first ring by a robotic voice. "Mr. Louis you have approximately 20 minutes to get in front of the Barclay Center and go to the last payphone to the right. A number will be taped on the top. Call the number if not; the images you just saw will be released to the press and your daughter will be killed. Do not call the police."

"Who is this?" he asked.

The phone hung up leaving him nervous and he didn't have much time. Traffic at 6 p.m. would be brutal trying to get back to Brooklyn. He was about to call the police but stopped immediately he remembered the voice said not to. He called the one person he knew he could trust.

BARCLAYS CENTER

Robert pulled up to the Barclay Center with about 45 seconds to spare. He jumped out and looked for the payphones. He saw the one he was looking for and sprinted to it. He found the number taped to the inside of the phone and called.

"Very well Mr. Louis. I am glad you made it."

"Who is this? What do you want?"

"Who I am is not important, but what I want is 100 million wired to the account taped under the phone you just called me from. If funds are not transferred within 48 Hours your daughter will be dead and your company will be shut down. Do you understand?" the voice said.

"Yes. Where is my daughter?"

The line hung up and he reached into his pocket to grab his cell to call Korina, but he got no answer. He called her assistant, but she hadn't seen her either. He called Amelia who was at Korina's apartment, but she said she didn't come home last night and she hasn't heard from her. His heartbeat became faster as he saw some NYPD officers nearby. No cops he remembered. He thought about Dan and called his number, but the number went to voicemail. He needed to think and think quick. His phone rang.

"Hello?"

"Yo bro I'm at your spot, where are you?"

"Stay there I'm on my way" he hung up and jumped in the SUV.

PURE LOUNGE

Robert explained all that happened to Fite who sat attentively. He knew if he could talk with anyone it would be him. When Robert finished explaining Fite got on the phone with Wade, his IT guy because he thought he could help. He told Robert to go on about his day and he will call him as soon as he had some information.

So many thoughts ran through his head. He never thought he would be in such a situation. Then again, he knew that success could attract such individuals. The only problem with that was that the individuals didn't know that once he was pissed off all bets were off. Drew came and asked him if he wanted something to drink. He had him make a vodka straight.

"Everything okay boss?"

"Yes, just one of those days when there is always something. You know what I mean?"

"I sure do...happens all of the time in my world."

"So, what is your solution?" Robert asked.

"Well, I have two actually" Drew said placing his palms on the bar."

"Let's hear it."

"Blow jobs and comedy" Drew said with a smile.

Robert nearly choked on his drink. Drew handed him a napkin and made him a glass of water.

"Jesus."

"Not what you expected I'm guessing" Drew asked.

"Definitely not what I was expecting but that's what I get for asking," Robert said.

"That's the thing with questions."

"What's that?" Robert asked.

"You never know the answer you're going to get when you ask" Drew said looking at Robert with an unsuspecting inviting expression.

Robert cleared his throat, took the rest of the shot, and had Drew pour him another. His phone rang, and he went back to his desk. It was Fite.

"That was fast. What do you got?"

"I know. Where are you?"

"Still at my office. Why?"

"Get out now and meet me at mine," Fite said urgently.

"Okay," he hung up.

"Everything alright boss?" Drew asked.

Robert just looked at him, grabbed his things, and left.

FITE'S CIGAR BAR & LOUNGE

Robert got to Fite's momentarily as he had to source the capital for the ransom. He didn't know if he was going to have positive feedback. So he made sure he would at least have the money ready for the drop. Fite had Wade run a trace on the USB drive. Wade didn't get a name, but he did lift the longitude and latitude off the cell phone image of one of the photos.

The coordinates linked back to a burner phone which could be traced back to a location in Harlem. Robert wanted to go himself but couldn't as he was too recognizable. Fite would have lent his people given he was a Mason, but Masons could only assist Masons with this kind of situation. He remembered some guys from prison he could call that wouldn't mind this kind of action. He left Fites, got into his SUV, and made the call.

JACKSONVILLE, NORTH CAROLINA

"**H**ello."

"Matt! What's up its Robert."

"Robert who?"

"Robert Louis from the fed man 058."

"Oh, shit my nigga what is up? Damn, I was just fuckin talkin' 'bout your ass man damn what's up my nigga?"

"Don't call me nigga. I'm not a nigga."

"Damn it's like that nigga? Damn. We ain't even on it like that black man" Matt said.

"I'm not black either I'm African-American I done told you. Don't make me give you another lesson about melanin."

"Stop it. You's a nigga black man. Don't be like that but what's up though?"

"I need your help with something important."

"Shit what's up? Holla at me then" Matt said attentively.

"Can't talk over the phone. How soon can you get to New York?"

"I could be on the first thing smokin as long as you paying. You know a brother pockets kind of tight and shit my nigga but if you say we ridin then we motherfukin ridin shit, you know what I'm saying?"

"Okay. Where is Deuce?"

"Right here big sensitive and shit, talking to some chick. You want to holler at him?"

"No just tell him..."

"Hold on...Deuce, bruh on the phone man" Matt said in the background.

"Who?" the voice said in the distance.

"Bruh man 058 stop playing you know who bruh is man damn don't be like that."

"Be like what? Hell bruh can be anybody" the voice said sounding closer.

Robert couldn't believe he was calling Matt and Deuce, but he had no one else he trusted. They all met in federal prison and had each other's back. Matt was a 5'4 mulatto in denial of having a short man complex that kept him angry all of the time. He was short but made it up with impeccable strength and had the heart of a lion. He was the type who will beat you to death, just so he could feel bigger. Deuce was the complete opposite standing at 6'3 235 lb. and dark-skinned. He was as wide as a mature oak tree and had log massive arms. He and Matt would argue constantly about any and everything. He also knew that hiring them would mean most of the time they would be arguing.

"Man take the phone man damn don't be like that" he heard Matt yell.

"Hello," Deuce said.

"What's up man it's Robert."

"Oh, hell man what's up? Why didn't he just say it was you on the phone shit I would have been got it. Matt stupid" Deuce said in a calm tone.

"I did tell you. I said bruh on the phone damn" Matt said from a distance.

"Yeah but you ain't say Robert though you said bruh," Deuce said slightly away from the phone.

"Man, we not gone do this now," Matt said from a distance.

"Deuce?" Robert called getting his attention because if not he and Matt would just argue and forget he was on the phone.

"Yeah, I'm here what's up?"

"I need you and Matt to get on the first flight to New York in the morning. I got some work for you two okay?"

"Okay, that's what's up. Here go Matt."

"Yooooo" he answered.

"Matt?"

"Yeah, what's up my nigga?"

"Don't call me nigga man I done told you. I'm going to kick your ass man."

"Daaaaaamn when we start doing it like that? Thought you was all black peace and shit. Thought we was friends, damn nigga."

"We are not friends Matt we are associates. There is a difference."

"Gotdamn man shit that's fucked up nigga," Matt said knowingly irritating Robert.

"Matt!" Robert shouted, now aggrieved.

"I'm just fucking with you black man so what's up with the details?"

Robert gave him the details and waited on his associates to show up in New York.

MONTVILLE TOWNSHIP NEW JERSEY

R obert sat in his home office looking out the window hoping Korina was okay. So much had happened he couldn't understand how all this was even present in his life, but he could feel the old him surfacing. He did all he could to suppress his urges to be angry and aggressive.

His associates from prison arrived that morning and were already on the way to the location that was given to them by Fite's IT guy. They argued a lot, but they could be very effective guys when it came to getting things done. Robert could almost still smell the fresh blood that poured out the inmate's neck that had a run-in with Matt and Deuce on the yard.

He was supposed to be a tough guy but by the time the medical staff got to him, he was just some punk who had just pissed himself as the rigor mortis set in. Robert saw the whole thing but when questioned said nothing and he was respected for that. Truth be told he wanted to shed a good amount of blood himself. He had a chip on his shoulder that was the size of a boulder. Even after his release, success, and having his life back something deep inside wanted revenge on the guy who placed him in prison. He prayed endlessly to not be angry and have negative energy and it worked...almost.

Finding out he was a father gave him a new sense of pride and dignity he didn't know he had. How insanely fast his protective instincts came to him was shocking. He wanted her to have the world although she was a little much to handle, he admired how relentless she was for finding him. Accomplishing all she had not giving up he saw so much of himself in her. The sure hunger of wanting something better out of life and not submitting to societies American dream of generational debt.

Not envying what someone else has, and having the guts to find out how to get it yourself is what life was about. Conquering one's fears, and achieving ones goals are how you got to the top. You want something you immerse yourself into getting it. Yes, she was his daughter and he was grateful that she went through what she did to be recognized. She was a true Louis. He was lighting a cigar when the main line rang. What he heard infuriated him as he instructed Matt to meet him at his warehouse in the Bronx. They were successful in not only finding who it was that sent images, but they kidnapped them too.

SOUTH BRONX NEW YORK

The warehouse in the Bronx was a place Robert intended to use as a pop-up location for rave parties when he could get around to doing some major cleaning. It was infested with rats and had a lot of roof damage. For the moment it was good as any place for Matt and Deuce to apply relentless pain for a very unlucky individual who no doubt was present at their death site.

"Yo, ain't no way black chicks got shit on a white girl" Matt protested.

"Man, you're crazy. Black women have better asses than white women."

"White women asses be all skinny and shit" Deuce rebutted.

"Stop man now you lieing man you ever see Jennifer Lawrence's ass man? That ass is like that bruh now come on."

"Who the hell is Jennifer Lawrence?" Deuce asked.

"Oh, we not going to do that now," Matt said offended picking through an assortment of nails. "She played in

'The Hunger Games'" Matt said pushing a nail to the side.

"Ahhh shit! She cute but her ass ain't fat."

"Stop man you're in denial boy that snow bunny is like that bruh come on now," he said reaching out for Deuce to shake his hand.

Deuce waved Matt's hand off then sent a punishing right hand into the forehead of the guy sitting in the chair knocking him and the chair over. The guy grunted great agony.

"How many is that?" Matt asked.

"I'm about to glove you," Deuce said.

"Shit ain't no way. I'm up in this joint" Matt boasted.

"No, you ain't man, you only knocked him down two times to my four. One more and that's the glove."

"See we not even gonna do that Deuce. You trying to cheat" Matt said shaking his finger smiling.

"How am I cheating Matt look at the nails. How many nails I got?"

"3."

"Bullshit man you cheating now you know I got 4 nails man. Look let's ask him."

The two men looked at the man in the chair that was bleeding from a cut to his eye, mouth, and cheek. He was crying looking between the men who were beating him.

"Yo how many times I knock you over in the chair 3 or 4?" Deuced asked.

The man just looked at him scared and shocked the guys were even using his face for a punching contest.

"Look man once I glove him it's over. Just tell him so we can get on with our other business" Deuce said.

The guy was still scared but hoping the bigger guy was right about going to other businesses, so he gave into the men.

"4," the man said.

"See I told you, Matt. I want my 25 push-ups too" Deuce said feeling triumphant.

"How? That's it, I ain't bout to do this stupid ass shit man. The motherfucka lieing' man shit."

"How he going to tell me how many times I knocked him over in the chair?"

"Because he is the motherfucka gettin' knocked the fuck over," Deuce said.

"Ain't no way. We got to do something else man I'm not getting gloved."

"Oh, that's some bullshit man. You mad I'm winning, now you want to quit. You are a sore loser."

"Man, I'm not it's just this bitch ass nigga tryin' to get out of this shit so we got to start doing something else."

"Damn man you ain't shit for that. I was winning now you want to kill the game and do something else" Deuce said waving Matt off in disgust.

"No, I just know we supposed to be asking questions because bruh on his way over here."

"So, ask some questions then, but your ass still owe me 25 push-ups or I'm going to knock your ass out."

"See that's what we not going to do right there. Ain't no way" Matt said squaring off with Deuce.

"Man ask the questions. Damn! You sore loser."

"Call me what you want but you won't call me gloved ha!" Matt laughed.

Matt picked up a rope that was 30 inches long and about 3 inches thick with a knot at the tip. He grabbed the straight end in his right hand, then drew back to hit the man in the chair.

"Wait!" Deuce said. "Use the socks with the rocks in it."

311

"Why? I like the rope."

"The knot is loose. You hit him it's gonna come undone."

"Ok I got something better."

"What?" Deuce asked.

"Deez nuts," Matt said laughing out loud hard.

"Man, that shit is gay as hell smh."

"C'mon bro don't be like that now come on."

"Hurry man we ain't got all day."

"Aight! Aight! Aight!" Matt said laughing.

He picked up a large oversized monkey wrench and hit the man in the kneecap.

When Robert showed up to the warehouse he could barely see the face of the guy in the chair for it was covered in blood and badly swollen. The man began to cry even more when he saw Robert come through the door. His body convulsed all over and he began to plead for his life. Deuce and Matt looked at Robert as he starred at Drew his bartender. The two men looked at each other as if they were hiding something.

"Well? What did he say? Where is my daughter? Is she safe?"

Deuce and Matt look at each other again.

312

"What is it? What did he say?" Robert demanded.

"It's your daughter bro," Matt said.

"What about her? What did he do to her?" Robert was shaking. He could feel his eyes sting from tears welling up in them.

"No bro he's saying she's behind this shit man," Deuce said.

"What do you mean she is behind it?"

"I mean she set all this up and been having him keep tabs. Look at this."

Deuce open a laptop they got from Drew that had a video of Kim doing cocaine with Korina in front of a hidden camera to set her up, so she could lose the part. He even had a recorded conversation from Domingo and Kim the night she died. The images of allowing under aged girls into the club came from him that he got off a website. He planned to use them to stir the press with the girl's parents to get the lounge shut down. Robert was blazing mad. He could feel his adrenaline rush. Everything turned orange.

"Why?" Robert asked looking at Drew. "Why would you do this to me?"

"Because you didn't see me. I would have done anything for you and you treated me like a regular worker."

"What the fuck?" Matt said.

"Aye yo," Deuce said grinning.

"What are you talking about?" Robert asked Drew.

"Ever since I heard your story I've been a fan. I idolized you. I showed up at the places you spoke at and applied for the jobs you had. I worked around and got good with Michael by getting him fine girls, so he got me a job. That's when I met Korina and she told me her intent. I wasn't going to go through with it though" Drew cried.

"Why because you got caught?"

"No!"

"Then why?"

"Because."

"Because! What?" Robert asked.

"Because I love you" Drew broke down.

"Gotdamn he a cupcake" Matt said.

"Ooooooooooohhh shit bro, that's craaaazzzzyyy bruh damn it's like that? Tell me it ain't like that bruh damn" Matt said laughing.

"Damn man that's fucked up man," Deuce said.

Robert couldn't believe what he just heard. His own daughter tried to extort him. How in the world could this be happening to him? His own flesh and blood treating him like a stranger. He had an attorney make her his beneficiary so if something happened his $4.7 billion estate would go to her. Now she would get nothing. Korina was complicated but he didn't think she was evil. So now he would have to figure out how to deal with her. He knew good and well what he was going to do.

"What you want us to do with him?" Deuce asked.

"Bruh! This man, boy, girl, whatever just said he loves you now you can't go out like that bro. Talk to me what are we doing?" Matt asked.

Robert thought about Kim, and then he thought about Jenna. It was Korina who led Justine to Jenna's house based on what Drew had.

"Kill him" he said.

"Myyyy boooyyeee. Yeah, that's your ass fruit cake" Matt said.

315

"No! No! No! Please don't please don't Robert. Don't kill me, please. I'll tell you where Domingo is please don't kill me" Drew pleaded.

"Wait what did you just say? You know where Domingo is?" Robert asked.

"Yes, and I'll tell you, but please don't kill me."

"Where is he?" Robert demanded.

"Promise you won't kill me please."

"I promise to kill you if you don't. Now where is he?"

"No, give me your word you won't kill me." Robert pondered on it for a second.

"Okay, I will not kill you."

"Man fuck that bro. Now I ain't tryna to tell you how to handle your business..." Matt said.

Robert cut him off "Then don't," he said harshly. "Where is he, and where is Korina?"

"Domingo is in the Isle of Palms South Carolina, and Korina is in Bedminster New Jersey" Drew said.

"Man, this some shit right here man you should let me smoke this fool" Matt pled.

"So be it" Robert responded.

"No! You said you wouldn't!" Drew contested looking at Robert.

"I'm not...they are." Robert turned to walk away and all you could hear were gunshots.

CHARLESTON SOUTH CAROLINA

Downtown Charleston was alive and well with tourists pouring from all of the Carnival-type ships that were docked just across from the battery. With its timeless southern charm, it illuminated with historical monuments of architecture and pride. From corner sold boiled peanuts, fresh oysters, to the Red Hat Club; Charleston pioneered the South for their amazing experience, beauty, and disposition of culture. You could find many people taking the horse and buggy rides, buying from the large market, or dining in fine Cajun cuisine restaurants that could get a 5-star rating on its worst day. For the water bugs, the ocean sat waiting, an abundance of fun for catching the fairies and seeing the dolphins swim to the pier around 7 a.m.

Robert couldn't help taking in a place that changed his life so much. He told himself he would move to Charleston in 2011 but ended up falling for Meghana so he decided to move back to North Carolina. He never felt at home from the day he arrived in Huntersville nor would it ever remind him of a great place now that they were divorced. He made a mental note to never go to another place for a woman again. Fool him twice shame on him and all. Even though he was there to find

Domingo he couldn't help but be somewhat excited to be headed back to the Isle of Palms since that is exactly what made him fall in love with Charleston in the first place.

'Twas one of the most romantic summers he ever had in his life with this beautiful woman he met named Constance from Nicaragua. She was the daughter of a former baseball player who was drafted by the Phillies back in the seventies. He was on vacation and she was there for her best friend's wedding. He was walking with the rest of the tourists on the USS Yorktown when he spotted her in the wedding rehearsal dinner. She was 5'11, 140 lbs. with mile-long legs and what seemed like a perfect tan given she was white and Nicaraguan. Her hair was styled short and curly in a small afro. They conversed for a while ultimately spending the whole week together.

He remembered walking on the beach with her and eating at Poes one late rainy evening. They visited the Boone Hall Plantation together comparing African history to Nicaraguan history. Both noticed how the local African Geechee Charlestonians only worked on the Isle of Palms and didn't live there. It was one of the main reasons he wanted to move there. As he was crossing the Arthur Raven Junior Bridge connecting Charleston to Mount Pleasant he wondered where

319

Constance was in life and if she was doing well. She probably was happily married with children. He was happy to be back in Charleston after so many great memories he had there.

Robert made yet another call to an associate he made while in the federal system by the name of Mafia. Mafia was from Connecticut but had family in nearby Georgetown. He had Mafia do some recon in the area and found exactly where Domingo was staying. He was headed to meet Mafia at Poes to discuss the details and give Deuce and Matt the word to move in on Domingo.

Although his associates were capable he had to keep in mind Domingo was more vicious now on the run than anything. He also needed to move quickly because he knew that Detective Nick Morales and the FBI were not too far off. Chaz told him Morales came back to the lounge, and one of the waitresses that dated Domingo said he had ties to Myrtle Beach. Even though it was some ways off it wouldn't be long before they filtered his location to Charleston.

POES RESTURANT

"Boy the snow bunnies is all out here man damn look at that one right there" Matt said sounding like a kid in a candy store.

"Oh, so you finally embracing your white side?" Deuce asked.

"You damn right cause if it ain't white it ain't right" he laughed.

"Boy stop. Now her right there she okay for a white girl" pointing at a waitress serving a table just past the left of the bar.

"Man, she is like that but look at her" Matt said pointing to a waitress coming out of the kitchen.

"Damn she is definitely like that. She got to be from an island. 25 pushups she from like Hawaii or something" Matt said.

"Nah man, she Mexican...and bet" Deuce accepted.

"Bet. Excuse me beautiful. May I ask you a question?" Matt and Deuce smiled as the exotic-looking waitressed approached.

Mafia and Robert viewed them from the back of the restaurant.

"Man, why you bring those two with you man? Out of all the people you could have brought you got them two" Mafia said looking at Deuce and Matt invite a waitress over.

"Hey, they were the ones that volunteered, and they actually did well with something I had up in NY, so yeah, this was a no-brainer."

"I hope you're right because dude, that man big as shit. I thought he was going to be like a little nigga or something. Man, that motherfucka like 6'9 or some shit. What Matt lil ass gone do to that big ass dude?"

"He can handle himself pretty good and I'm sure he got his toolbox, so I'm not concerned with that much."

"Matt lil ass better have two toolboxes shit; he gone look like an infant standing next to that big ass nigga. Deuce might have a chance but Matt lil ass gone get knocked the fuck out" Mafia started laughing.

"Well I hope it doesn't lead to that, but you know how it goes," Robert said.

"Yeah, unfortunately, I do. I would pay 1,000 stamps to see that shit though damn."

"Not stamps Mafia we're not on the yard anymore," Robert said laughing.

"I know but that's how serious that shit would be though."

"So where is my little friend anyway?"

"He's out in the IOP at the Wild Dunes Resort in one of those condos off the golf course. It has a guard entrance, so I got some people who would give you access from the clubhouse, then you can take the south entrance." Mafia pointed at a diagram of the resort layout explaining another route if needed.

"Why the south entrance? What's wrong with this west entrance here?" Robert pointed by a body of water.

"Crocodiles all in that pond man. There are signs all through there and I wouldn't want you to go crawling through and get your asses chewed off."

Looking at the layout Robert knew exactly where Domingo was staying as it was right behind the condo Constance was staying at the night he slept with her. He remembered how they saw the same signs on the balcony while drinking Flor De Cana imported from Nicaragua. Robert thought to himself how beautiful Constance was and how her body was so sexy. Even after all those years she still put a smile on his face. He

323

was still smiling as he saw Matt doing pushups on the floor in the restaurant while the waitress and Deuce laughed.

ISLE OF PALMS WILD DUNES RESORT

3 A.M.

Domingo heard a noise in the living room of the condo. His instincts kicked in immediately and he pulled out his Glock 9mm. Hearing the noise again he quickly placed on his shoes, slowly cocked his gun which was on safety, and eased to the door. He cracked the door, but his view was partially impaired by the corner wall in the hallway. If he wanted a better angle, he would have to go out on the balcony from his room then over to the sliding doors which opened into the living room. Or he could go to the bathroom which opened into the hallway. The living room sliding doors were locked as he locked them every night. The bathroom was his only option so he crept quickly as the noise in the kitchen continued.

Whomever it was, was opening doors, so apparently, they were there trying to rob him. Not tonight he thought. Definitely the wrong night, and the wrong guy. He walked into the bathroom, tip-toeing to the center his massive frame made the floor squeak. It wasn't loud, but it seemed to have echoed in his head. Not only that but when he paused, so did the noise in the living room.

Seconds later, it started again so he tip-toed to the door and pushed it open just enough to see the living room. He could see a figure moving about in the moonlight through the long plantation blinds. He figured he only had seconds before whoever it was made their way to the bedroom. He opened the door as the figure went into the kitchen. He heard the rattling of silverware. "Dumb fuck about to die over some cheap silver", he felt confident.

Robert was already at the front door in the shadows when he saw the bathroom door open a bit. He also could see Deuce holding his gun at the bathroom door as he made little noises. Knowing Domingo will be armed, he had his vest on, ready for whatever.

Matt was stepping with Domingo as he stepped in the bathroom just behind him. He was not even two steps away when Domingo entered the hallway. He saw how Domingo's posture was broader than it had previously been. He knew that Domingo thought that he was being robbed, and just like a big and tall guy, he will underestimate what a guy his height could do, but he sure as hell well was about to find out. Right, when Domingo hit the corner, Robert hit the light, blinding him and Matt delivered a vicious kick from behind him to his balls. When he bent over, Deuce stepped through following his 45mm and hit Domingo right across his

326

temple. The gun flew out of his hand, allowing Matt the perfect shot at his jaw, in which he landed a clean shot with a metal pole. Domingo was out cold

When Domingo came to he was tied to a chair at the kitchen table with a blurry view of Robert Louis reading a newspaper. His head felt as if it had been slapped by a phone book in the hands of Lou Ferrigno. His blurred vision was clearing when he saw Robert Louis taking a sip of coffee. He thought he also smelled breakfast.

"Hope you don't mind we helped ourselves while you were out. You're out of juice by the way."

"Yeah, you definitely out of juice nigga. How the fuck you gon' have like a half corner in a container of juice? You a big ass nigga you should've just drank that shit and took your ass to the store. I hate that shit" Matt said to Deuce.

"You just mad you ain't get none" Deuce replied.

"Shit, I may have if this fuckknuckle would've went to the store, but I got me some coffee, so a nigga straight though, you know what I sayin'?" Matt sipped his coffee.

"Yeah whatever you mad you ain't get no juice"

"No, what I'm mad at, is that you ain't give me my 25 pushups yet. I need them joints you know what I sayin?"

"Damn you not even gone let me finish my food?" Deuce looked at Matt aggravated.

"Yeah go ahead and eat, I ain't even gone be like that my nigga, go ahead black man"

Robert sat looking at Domingo for a second pondering what he should do to him. Being in South Carolina presented so many choices, from the ocean, swamps, woods, old abandoned farms, abandoned homes, and the list went on and on. He was thinking of Kim, and with every thought, he wanted to go medieval on him. Domingo was gagged so he couldn't scream. Robert made sure he was awake long enough to know who had him before he was knocked out again.

"It's time," he said.

Deuce placed chloroform on a rag and covered Domingo's nose and mouth. Domingo's vision blurred looking at Robert holding a newspaper.

MONTVILLE TOWNSHIP NEW JERSEY

Domingo woke up in a large king-size bed with a massive headache. He was still wearing the same clothes groggy from the chloroform he was exposed to earlier. He attempted to gather his bearings but his mind was still cloudy. One thing that was apparent was that Robert Louis found out where he was and if he had him there was no escape.

He tried to come up with a solution to buy some time, but he had no way of knowing where he was. 'Sun' he thought looking at the window that was clean with no bars or cage. He looked at the bed he was in. Even the room looked modern and immaculately kept. There was water beside the bed and even his gun.

As he reached for it a piercing pain shot through his groin. He remembered how something hit him between his legs right before he was knocked out. He checked his gun and it was empty. He got up to look out of the window and immediately knew where he was by recognizing the black SUV. It was the same SUV he had driven and rode in many times before. He knew he was at Robert Louis's home. He couldn't figure out nor wrap his head around what was going on, but the door opened to do just that.

"Good. You're up. I thought I heard you stirring"

"Huh?" He said discombobulated. Robert pointed to what looked like a baby monitor.

"Hungry?" Robert asked.

"More like hurting Boss" he replied

"No...don't say a single word. There are clothes and fresh towels for you in the bathroom. Get cleaned up and meet me downstairs." Robert said then turned and walked out the door.

Domingo was confused but he felt relieved at how he was being treated. It gave him a sign of hope. Hope that he'd been praying for. He got up, showered, put on the jumpsuit, and went downstairs.

"Look! Look! Alessandra or Kendall?" Matt asked.

"Alessandra."

"Ain't no way, come on man stop playing be real."

"Alessandra looks better than Kendall. Don't ask me then get offended shit" Deuce said.

"I'm not offended I just can't see it, man. Kendall is like that bruh."

"She aight but she, not Alessandra."

"Yeah, I'll give you that one. What about Kate Hudson or Katie Holmes?"

"Who?" Deuce asked.

"Kate Hudson or Katie Holmes?"

"Let me see." Deuce stopped playing the game to look at the Us magazine Matt was reading.

"Shit both," Deuce said resuming his game.

"I know right them some bad snow bunnies."

"Shit where the black girls' man you always looking at them white people's magazines. Why?"

"Because," Matt said flipping through the pages.

"Because what?"

"Damn nigga why you acting like that?"

"You can't even answer the question."

"It ain't that I can't. I just don't choose to."

"Ummm hmmm you black and white and you are the most racist person I know," Deuce said as he shifted his attention back to the video game.

"Now we ain't gone to do that now," Matt said trying to slap the controller out of Deuces hands.

331

"He in his office. He said grab something to eat and meet him in there" Deuce said catching Domingo in the corner of his eye.

Matt put the magazine down, stood, and starred at Domingo as if he was prepared to do battle. Domingo just walked to Robert's office and Matt followed.

Robert's office looked like a mini version of the Oval Office in the White House. It had the KPNC logo in the center on black carpet with white decal. He sat at the large black desk in a buttoned-up shirt with the tie missing, and his sleeves rolled up exposing his prison tattoos he had done by Eli.

"Have a seat" he gestured to Domingo.

"Thanks. Boss I..." Robert held up a finger cutting him off.

"The only reason you're breathing right now is because I want to hear for myself what happened. I'm still very well capable of having my two associates make you disappear. Tell me what happened the night Kim died. If you lie... If I remotely think you're lying I will make you feel pain that will last longer than the genocide of blacks in America. You can talk now" Robert said coldly.

"Kim and I had some sort of agreement. I would supply her and sometimes she and I will have sex. I truly liked her. I actually loved her. When she was doing the movie,

I knew my shot was over and I accepted it. That was until the video came out showing her doing coke when she announced she was pregnant and lost the movie. I didn't sell her that coke she OD'd on and I don't know where it came from. When she called me to the hotel that night I made my last run and was out of supply, but I still went to see her. When I got there, she was already high. I asked her what she doing getting high knowing she was pregnant. She told me it was going to be her last time and she was just in a funk but was trying to figure things out.

See we had talked about her mom and about how she felt alone after Jenna was shot. She said she felt bad for not calling Jenna that night instead of going to some meeting. She felt had she called Jenna, Jenna would have come to her and she wouldn't have been shot. She was really beaten up about it. I told her how I felt and that I would help her through it. She was feeling sick that night and I told her she shouldn't have taken that dope. We fell asleep and when I woke up she was gone. I called her name and checked the bathroom door.

It was locked. I knocked and knocked. I was about to break it, but my cell phone rang. It was Ireland trying to reach me to get to the gym. Not thinking I grabbed my things and left...figured I'd call her later. I didn't make it to Ireland's house because my connect needed to meet with me, so I bailed out on my workout and rushed to meet my connect. That's the honest-to-god truth."

"Did you give Kim more powder that night?" Robert asked him coldly.

"No. I swear I had nothing on me that night I swear."

"Then where did she get the dope?"

"I don't know but it wasn't from me. I didn't even know she had more because her black compact was empty when I got there. I don't even know where she got that because I hadn't supplied her in months. I swear to you, boss I loved Kim. I wouldn't have had given her dope while she was pregnant" he said with tears in his eyes.

Robert sat and looked at Domingo pondering. He leaned to the phone and said "Okay". As soon as he did detective Morales walked in the door. Domingo's heart sank into his stomach because he knew he was about to go to jail forever.

HAMPTON NEW YORK

3 WEEKS LATER

As Robert poured another shot of vodka, Jenna set at the counter in tears. She couldn't help but feel how abandoned Kim must have been having to go through that alone. She wished that she could have been there for her friend to comfort her and let her know everything would have been okay. Why couldn't she have not answered the door that night? If she didn't she could have been there for Kim. Even though Domingo had been found, it still did not change how bad she felt about her friend.

Her friend who was pregnant that would never get to hold her own child. A friend that would never get to be a mother. A friend she would never get to smile and laugh with again. Robert walked around to where she was and held her. She cried so hard on his shoulder and he just remained strong for her. With every tear that fell from Jenna's eyes his anger grew and his vision went from seeing orange to seeing red... "God help me," he said to himself conceding to the rage. He began to hold Jenna tighter.

PURE LOUNGE

3 MONTHS LATER

Pure was on fire with the hottest of the hottest in all Industries. Robert stood at his mirrored glass and looked out at all the people enjoying themselves. Thinking just months ago his life was completely out of control from finding out he had a daughter, to losing a friend, to security detail changes, to reaching out to people he met while he was in prison, the FBI all over his lounge, and his brother being beaten. Wow, how life can change in an instant he thought. He was remembering how his celly SK would always tell him "The one thing that you can always count on is change." He told himself to remember that.

He needed to reach out to his old celly as well to check up on him and his new godson. SK met his old assistant and they hit it off. Now they were married and expecting their first child together. He liked happy moments like that. Pleasurable imagery as SK would call it. It was almost time for him to do his rounds when he turned around to see Amelia coming in the door with Jenna. Jenna was holding Amelia's arm because Amelia was pregnant with Roberts's daughter whom they decided to call Kimberly. He smiled at the sight of them. He turned to look back out at the floor and saw Domingo by the bar handling some minor issues with a guy.

He thought about the day he heard the recording of Domingo and Kim that fateful day in the hotel. He knew Domingo was innocent and all charges were dropped. He knew from what Drew told him that it was Korina who had been the one who somehow tainted the cocaine Kim sniffed. Robert looked at Amelia talk to Jenna. He knew that she would never see Korina again as her head was in the Hudson, her torso was in Victoria Texas, and her legs were in Manhattan Beach California.

His vision was clear as ever now and he felt great about his future, a future with his new family, and great friends. Yes, everything was going to be alright. He straightened his suit and set out to speak to Detective Morales and his lady friend who was his honored guests. He smiled and walked out of his office.

"Look! Look! Damn, she smoking boy the bunnies is up in this joint" Matt said rubbing his hands together.

"Shut up man you're supposed to be checking names, not the chicks you're gonna get us fired."

"I'm checking the names, I'm pulling all of them up on my Tuvuler account adding all them bunnies."

337

"Matt don't none of these chics want you, you're trippin'" Deuce said.

"Why cause I'm a black man?"

"You're not black Matt. You're mulatto."

"Stop it! You acting like I can't pull none of these chics. Aight next bunny walk up I'm bagging her watch" he said confidently.

"Aight bet 25 push-ups for the next chic that walks up if you don't get the number," Deuce said.

"Bet! This is too easy, watch your boy go to work. Here we go! Here we go! Yeeeaah this all me."

"Name please?"

"Sharon Osbourne," she said.

"Okay, Sharon Osbourne. Let me see...your name ain't on here but if you pass me the number I got you, you know what I sayin'?" Matt said looking smiling at Deuce.

She busted out laughing and walked past him. As she walked off she told her friends "I must tell Robert adding little comedians at the door is a really nice touch."

"Ooooooohhh," Deuce said holding his fist over his mouth laughing. Matt turned red. "You owe me 25 push-ups" Deuce laughed.

"Yo! Hell no Sharon Osbourne disrespectful as shit. We ain't even doing that."

REASON 10

HE'S A BABY

———— o ————

How many times in your life have you been in a situation where you ask yourself "Self? Why in the hell did I do that?" And your mind will respond "I have no idea." Nothing in life poses that question more than the experience of being in overly committed relationships. Relationships you just devote extremely too much time and energy into with nothing in return. There is a saying that goes "Take your own best advice." Well if you're reading this book right now I want you to focus on what I am about to say, and I really need you to give this particular cheater your utmost attention.

He is the most common cheater, the most alluring cheater, and known for being the most abusive cheater. Not one single woman who is cheated on by a Baby walks around without some kind of scar. It could be emotional or physical. What makes the Baby cheater so alluring is that he keeps you in "Ahhh". "Ahhh you're so sweet." "Ahhh that was so nice." "Ahhh you shouldn't have." "Ahhh you're just so adorable." "Ahhh you are such a bad boy." He Ahhhs you all the way to motherhood. Motherhood is a state in a relationship where you are not only dating the Baby but you take care of him as well.

Case and point. You ever meet a guy who seems to have it all together in the beginning, car, home, dates, and conversation. Then all of a sudden, it's "I lost my job", "I have to move", "I wrecked my car", or "I'm short on cash, can you spot me?" Then you somehow end up with a roommate who you just so happen to be sleeping with. You convince yourself that it is alright because it's only a minor setback, it won't be long, he'll be closer, you don't want to be mean, and well let's face it, you will have "in house dick" available to you 24 hours a day ...Girl!. You just took in a man-child no two ways about it.

Women who are single mothers, who have low incomes, and are on dating websites have greater chances of dating the Baby. Just like the name, Baby is an undeveloped dependent when it comes to adulthood. He has spent his whole life not being responsible, and in his mind that is okay. A lot of them are mama's boys. I'm not talking about the mama's boy who can't let go of their mama's grasp. I mean the mama's boy who was in the conflicted household where the mama didn't allow the father to raise his son. A lot of women think that child support raises a young boy, and they couldn't be more wrong... But that's another situation.

341

Adulthood to Baby is like not getting his way, and what happens to a baby when it doesn't get what it wants? It lashes out into a tantrum. It yells at you, calls you nasty names, storms out, breaks things, won't communicate, won't respond, or even hits you. In Baby's case, he may even rape you.

This causes a lot of women to endure experiences that make them completely shut down, or just crawl into an emotional ball and give Baby what he wants. Then just like that, it becomes routine or common to the point where you accept it as normal behavior because you don't want the conflict or in some cases, you fear for your life.

Mentally Baby has had an experience that made him run away from being the man society needs him to be. Mainly not having his father or a legitimate male role model to properly influence him. He has allowed the experience to impact him emotionally so much that it beat him down from recovery. Baby needs help and it's going to take him to really hunker down to get it. Until that happens Baby will treat every relationship the same. If you are dating a Baby a true sign you are about to be left is the constant blowing up and arguing that gets him out of the house. In a way that's good for you because he will be gone but at what cost though? How much emotionally or financially are you willing to crawl

342

back from? Not only are you hurt but you're mad as hell too, isn't it better to just avoid it? What about her? The next woman he leaves you for. Make no mistake about it it's going to happen to her too.

You do ride an emotional rollercoaster with Baby. You lose a large amount of your individuality. You could be doing so much better without Baby. Try this out for a second. Ask yourself how many times you had this experience with relationships. Experiences where you ended up paying for meals, gas, and rent when you thought it was going to be a good relationship of interdependence.

Now add how many months from every experience you did this. Also add the amount of money you thought you would've had help with but ended up spending becasuse you supported him and you. What's the total amount? Now ask yourself if you had that money right now how better off would your life be?

Could you use it for that needed vacation? Buy a car, new home or just treat yourself to something nice? Yes! Yes! You could. Take your own best advice and save yourself the trouble of dating Baby. Because as soon as Baby says he has an issue and needs your help. You should say "Self what should I do?" And self should say "Ahhhh hell no. Girl run!"

TAINTED LOVE

M eghana McBride was sitting in front of the mirror
applying light makeup in her bathroom when she
received a text that said, "I'm home." It was a text she
had been receiving every day for the past week while
she was on spring break from teaching high school
English. It has been years since she was this excited
about meeting with a guy like the one she had met on
the dating site her roommate encouraged her to join.
She had been out of the dating scene for about 10 years
since the divorce from her ex-husband. Normally dating
sites were not her thing but she was glad that she joined
the one recommended.

It all started as a general conversation with a guy but it
finally led to her getting much attention, comfort, and
companionship she craved. As she looked in the mirror
she started to apply her eye shadow. The old clotted
blood residue from the busted vein in her eye was visible
still. As she looked at it, she stood back for a second but
told herself she wouldn't go down that road. Reaching
for her contact lens container she opened it. She
placed in her left contact before placing the second
contact on her right eye. When she was starting to lean
back she could smell Jim's alcoholic breath. The heat

from his heavy breathing was on her face. Her neck started to tighten as the feeling of his grip constricted around her throat and she couldn't breathe. She froze.

"Where are you going bitch? Huh? Where the fuck are you going, bitch?"

She was paralyzed. Her heart started to race, and it felt like the room was closing in on her. She saw him standing in the mirror looking at her. She slid down shaking from extreme fear covering her head because she knew the blow was coming like it always did. It felt as if her heart was going to beat out of her chest. Her mouth went instantly dry making it hard to swallow. She felt the blood swelling in her head. She couldn't breathe through her nose, so she clawed at his arm and tried to beat his hands loose.

"Please! Please!" she pleaded.

"Bitch!" he growled.

Knock! Knock! Knock!

The knock on the door sent a wave of air in her lungs while she was on the floor. She coughed and breathed in as deep as she could. She looked around and he was gone.

Knock! Knock! Knock!

Clearing her throat, she stood up. Her face was extremely pale.

"Yes?" she called out.

"I'm heading out do you need anything?" her roommate asked.

"No…no I'm fine thanks."

"Okay see you later."

She looked at herself in the mirror seeing she needed to touch herself back up. "He is not real you're fine. It's over" she told herself about 10 times. She had been battling that experience for years now and each time seemed get worse and worse. It was part of the reason she hadn't committed to anyone. She wanted to with her brother's friend from college but he seemed to never want to commit. Even their sexual arrangement allowed him have his cake and to eat it too. So when she started seeing Robert she didn't cut him off completely she just kept him in reserve. She got herself together then placed on her black cherry lotion from Bed Bath & Body Works. Giving herself one last look-over she prepared to leave.

ROCK HILL SOUTH CAROLINA

VILLAGE AT MANCHESTER APARTMENTS

2011

Robert's 1 bedroom 1-bathroom apartment was at the back of the village in Manchester Apartments which was located just five minutes from the movie theater. The local Rock Hill Recreation Park was just 20 yards across the street where during this time of year, spring female collegiate soccer teams would play games during the weekend at one of the nine soccer fields. It was a community of graduate students who attended Wingate College just down Cherry Road below the local auction center for cars. It was normally quiet during the afternoon, but for the last week around lunchtime, it sounded like a porno shoot

As Kevin Hart's "Big Little Man" played on the 42-inch plasma TV screen, bottles of Heinekens were perspiring on coasters on the wooden center table. The faded yellow couch that looked as if it had been in a freshman dorm for 12 years was occupied by Robert and Meghana. She had been laying her head in his lap when he started to become erect. She rubbed on him

347

and unbuttoned his True Religion jeans allowing his full erection to be completely exposed. Once out she leaned up just over it, allowed her spit to drop on the tip of the head, then stroked it with her hand. Once throbbing she took him into her mouth letting him enjoy every stroke.

She could feel him pulsating in her mouth so she stopped, slid his pants down to his ankles, reached over, grabbed her Heineken, took a sip, handed him the bottle then continued to suck him off. She continued until he couldn't take it anymore, so he lifted her, taking her into the bedroom.

He removed her shirt and she removed his. He took his left leg and stepped on his jeans to completely remove them from around his ankles. She was still stroking his penis in her right hand while massaging his balls with her left hand. He kissed her, rubbing her breasts while unhooking her bra from the front. As her bra open she removed her hands long enough for it to hit the floor and she continued to stroke his penis and balls. He was kissing her while gently, pinching her nipples before he slid off her black leggings.

Meghana didn't have any underwear on so he slid his right middle finger inside of her while standing at the side of the bed. He stepped on her leggings, allowing her to

348

remove them from around her ankles then laid her on the bed and took her slowly into his mouth.

She immediately responded by stroking her clitoris against his tongue and lips when he licked her vagina. It hadn't been 3 minutes that passed, and she was climaxing hard making her body convulse. He slid her all the way on the bed with her body lying across on her back. He entered her making her gasp as he stroked her hard, deep, and long. He grabbed the side of the bed with his left hand and her ass with his right hand. She spread her legs wider letting the heels of her feet sit on the back of his quads allowing him to enter deeper. He could hear her breathe in deep and as she started to climax he placed his lips on hers sucking her tongue and she moaned to the end.

Stroking her a couple more times she rolled him over and took him back into her mouth with her juices all over his penis. Robert started to shake because it was so sensitive but bared the feeling of sensation. He reached behind her and rubbed on her ass and she sucked on him faster whipping her head with every stroke. She stopped enough to mount him, take him inside her as she started to rock him back and forth. She laid on his chest, wrapping her arms around his neck and bounced up and down on his penis. He reached around placing his finger in her ass as she stroked his penis and finger at the same time. Stroking deeper and closer on him he started to climax grabbing her waist going deeper into her. They remained like that until they woke up from their nap.

HAMPTON UNIVERSITY

2002

Being from Valdosta Georgia Meghana was encouraged to attend Valdosta State along with the rest of her friends from high school. Wasn't much in the community outside of a mall, the college, and the military, so leaving was always an attractive perk for her. Her parents were wholesome people who had done what they could and were well-liked in the community. She would always remember that about them given that they were killed in a car accident when she was 12. She was raised by her aunt Nova since their death along with other family members.

Life wasn't bad, but it wasn't extravagant either. She had decent friends, made decent grades and had what most would consider a normal childhood in the small town. Yet with her parents gone she always felt like a burden to the rest of her family. Thus, when she was accepted by Hampton University she had emotionally detached from everything in Valdosta. Hampton would give her a chance to rewrite her life...a life which she and anyone who knew her could see had a major void.

Her dad was a plumber but he treated her like the world didn't spin unless she was happy. He was what a Dad was supposed to be to his daughter. Plenty of tickles, piggyback rides, funny dances, pick-ups to falls, brave when monsters were in the closet, and strong shoulder when trying to understand boys...protection from them anyway. He was why she always saw her mom smile and she no longer had that. Deep inside, she wanted them back so bad.

Meghana's first years at HU would give her a nice dose of what the world was like with so many personalities seeking to conquer it in deciding majors and minors. Hers was nursing. She made a considerable number of friends and even had a great love life with football jock Jim Jackson or JJ as everyone called them. He was from a small town out of Virginia and the son of a reverend. JJ had a side of him that all his friends and parents didn't know about. It was a sensitive side that brought Meghana and him closer than ever before. She felt proud when she and JJ got together because they made a beautiful couple. She - a cheerleader and he - a football player.

Everyone that saw them wanted to be with them. Even each of their friends had hidden feelings for them but no one dared to say anything because JJ had a temper and a severely bad drinking habit. That sensitive side could switch to rage anytime and Meghana was becoming all too familiar with it and also the bruises that came along. Meghana was very proud and even though she was being beaten by Jim she wouldn't let anyone know, not even her aunt and family.

Jim's parents almost seemed to hint they knew what was going on but never addressed it when they would visit for the holidays. As time passed, Jim was no longer attending school and left Meghana to pay the bills. He ended up getting caught by her for sleeping with one of her friends but instead of holding himself accountable he just blamed her and beat her while they argued.

When Meghana was pregnant with Haley she thought things would be different with Jim. Everyone was happy for them and was willing to help them with raising Haley since Meghana was still in school. Jim's football buddies would even come by and offer to help with babysitting. On the surface all was good but behind closed doors it was hell and they were about to lose their place again.

HUNTERSVILLE NORTH CAROLINA

2011

"Hey what's going on beautiful?"

"Hey, nothing much, what are you doing?"

"Sitting down here in Charleston with one of my clients and some others while they are out playing golf."

"You're not playing?"

"Nah I'm a contact sport kind of guy. I'm just here for the business deals."

"Haha, you and your business deals" she mocked.

"Yeah I know right?" he said playfully.

"Mr. Stay on the move."

"Hey, I'm going to slow down when I marry you though. I figured you can make an honest man out of me."

"Haha who said you were going to marry me?" she said cheerfully.

"I already know how things will end up between us watch."

"Oh yeah how do you know?"

"Because you're worth it, and a woman that is worth it should always be acknowledged with effort" he said.

These were the unique statements of confidence that made Meghana view Robert in another light. He was so passionate not only about life but passionate about her. Something no guy has ever made her feel before.

"When I get back we are going out on a date," he said sarcastically knowing he told her he would never take her on a date because he wanted to be different than the guys she had met before.

"Yeah, I hear you Mr. Go-On-A-Date. You have to be around to go on a date."

"I'm always around in spirit."

"I know I got something for your spirit Mr."

"I know you do" they both laughed.

"No for real when I get back we're going out okay?" he said seriously.

"I hear you," she said dismissively.

"I got you. I'll show you a good time out on the town. Dancing and all that."

All of a sudden, she broke the conversation to talk with Haley.

"Okay sorry, I'm back."

"Oh okay, where are you? Sounds like you're in the car."

"I am. I'm just sitting here so I can have peace of mind before everyone drives me crazy. My kids and my roommate's kids can be a little much."

"I bet, but you're doing a good job so don't forget to remember that. I know single moms don't get enough credit, but they should."

"I'm trying you know. I'm all they have" she said softly.

"You're all they need but who is there for you Meghana?" he asked.

She was happy she was on the phone so he wouldn't see her tear up as that is what she longed for, someone to just literally get it and deep down she knew he did. She knew he wasn't the kind of guy to abandon her.

JACKSONVILLE FLORIDA

2006

Meghana graduated from college and was working the night shift at Jacksonville Memorial Hospital as an RN. She and Jim just got married where she spent her honeymoon alone while he and his friends took a trip to New Orleans. She sat in the hotel with a bottle of champagne thinking about her future and where her life was heading with Jim.

She told herself over and over that she could make it work. The beatings were still happening as the drinking got worse. To make matters even more difficult Jim had gotten another woman pregnant at the same time as Meghana. She knew she should leave, but she didn't want to look like a failure to her family and she always thought you work through the marriage no matter what.

Jim had been trying to make money, but his drinking and drug use put them deeper in debt. Meghanas co-workers were tired of seeing her come to work with bruises and stood up for her. Many incidents left her beaten and raped in her apartment. When she came home on a Wednesday morning she walked into the apartment and the lights were off. Jim was still passed out from drinking. She thought to leave him at that very moment, but she didn't because she knew he would track her down. She sat at the table and cried as she looked for things to pawn.

Meghana longed for her parents so much because if they were around she would never be in this situation. How much longer would her life have to endure such ridicule and misery. Upset from crying she went to shower before contacting the electric company to see how much it would take to turn the lights on.

ROCK HILL SOUTH CAROLINA

2011

Robert had just had an extremely long day along with the 4-hour drive when he got home to his apartment. He had been working on sourcing investors for his principle which was taking more out of his pocket then it was putting in at the time. He knew things would pay off in the long run he just needed to stay at it. Any day now his ship will come in and he will be on top of the world.

Jumping in the hot shower did wonders for his sore back and he looked forward to getting a good night's sleep. When his phone rang he thought he was dreaming that he was about to be late for a conference call. It was about 10 p.m. when he answered the call from Meghana.

"Hey what's up?" he said sounding half asleep.

"Hey, I'm sorry were you sleeping?"

"No, I was just resting my eyes what's up?"

"Nothing just calling. Been having one of those days you know?"

"Oh yeah, what's up? You want to talk about it?"

"No, I will be alright I'm not going ruin your night with my issues."

"Not ruining anything. Talk to me you done woke me up now" he said laughing.

"Thought you said you weren't sleeping."

"I wasn't. I was resting my eyes, now tell me what's up."

"It's nothing really. How was your trip?"

"It was okay. Same old same old. Just driving around shaking my tin cup" he chuckled.

"Yeah I have a cousin that's a broker and he does good sometimes and then some time is not so good," she said.

"Tell me about it I feel like this is one of my not-so-good times but I'm sure it will pick up though."

Meghana started to say something when Haley came into her room asking why the water wasn't working. He could hear her telling Haley that it was off. He was getting dressed before she got back on the phone.

"Hey sorry about that," she said.

He didn't want to pretend he didn't hear what she said so he came out and asked her. "Hey, I couldn't help but overhear you tell Haley your water was off. Is there anything I can do?"

"Oh man, I'm sorry about that. No. It's fine I just forgot to pay the bill, so I will call them tomorrow it's no big deal" she said sounding slightly embarrassed.

It was a big deal to him as he was dressed, grabbing his wallet and on his way to her house. Robert grew up in a low-income housing project and was no stranger to no water or no lights. Hell, he even forgot to pay his cell phone bill at times. He knew Meghana was a proud woman but he would not sit back and do nothing. He was just getting on the highway. It would take about 45 minutes to get to her house.

"You sure I can't do anything? I can lend you the money if you need some. I really don't mind helping at all."

"Oh no...thank you, but no I will pay it in the morning," she said.

"What about baths and food?"

"I'll order them food and they will be okay until the morning."

"Are you sure?"

"Yes, I'm sure it's okay thank you."

"Okay," he conceited.

They talked for a while longer until he pulled up in her driveway. He rang her doorbell and told her to open the door.

"What?" she asked shocked.

"Open the door," he said.

"What in the world..." she said heading down the stairs. When she opened the door he was still on the phone.

"Hey, I was in the neighborhood."

"What are you doing here?" she asked hanging up the phone.

"Came to see a man about a horse. Hey, you got a Phillips head and some vice grips?"

"Yeah what for?"

"Grab them for me and meet me outside."

He walked out and backed up his truck in her driveway where her water meter was. When she came he took the Phillips's head and stuck it into the water valve. Using the vice grips, he turned the water back on. He covered the top and gave her the tools back and told her he will call her when he got back home.

VALDOSTA GEORGIA

2009

It had been some years since Meghana last saw Jim as he had brutally beaten her for the last time when he left scarred and never returned. He did call to plead his case but Meghana just wanted him to have a relationship with the kids. She had Cameron by herself because while she was giving birth Jim was with another woman. She didn't even care as she looked on the net to get documents and file for divorce. He was never notified. He just so happened to bring it up one day and she told him. There was nothing he could do.

She found a nice medium location between Valdosta and Virginia just in case his family wanted to see the kids which they never did. Even so she wasn't upset at any of them for his mistreatment of her. She was looking forward to starting over in North Carolina and had even been talking to Big G, a friend of a guy she considered her brother from college, who stayed in Charlotte. She looked at herself in the mirror and saw the busted vein in her eye. Never again she said.

HUNTERSVILLE NORTH CAROLINA

2013

"Babe come on" Robert called from downstairs.

Meghana was standing in the bathroom looking in the mirror as she washed her hands after she had just finished peeing.

"Okay I'm coming" she yelled back down.

"Woman you are slow. I promise you're going to be late for your own funeral."

"Leave me alone, I said I'm coming," she said.

Robert had Cameron and Haley get in her new SUV he just bought her after the car she had since college called "the fuck it bucket" broke down. He just went and got it after she said "Mama wants a new toy". He did so with no questions asked. He was a conqueror and the kids loved him. They loved him so much they wanted to change their last names to Louis since their dad wasn't in their lives and he was open to adopting them.

"Babe come on we're going to be late" he called again from downstairs at the front door.

"Okay! Okay! I'm coming" she said with a smile looking at the pregnancy test she just finished taking that informed her she was expecting.

Meghana was on top of the world as she had a new man, a new job, a new car, and a new lease on life.

THE END

LAST THING

⸻

I hope this was entertaining as much as it was eye-opening to reasons why men cheat. Truth is, a man will cheat for about any reason. I have a math equation that you can use to help you out. A - + a Man = Cheater. A negative plus a man equals a cheater...well, a reason he will cheat anyway. The one thing I've noticed is that women nowadays are not holding men accountable for being men anymore. Women are pacifying men and accepting male roles. It's not only devaluing men but it's devaluing women as well.

Men are becoming more and more disrespectful to women. Because of this, women are abandoning men for women and they're just eliminating them as a compatible companion to execute equally responsible relationships. Allowing men to call you wifey, and not making you his actual wife, is not only misleading it's just accepting inferiority. The millennial era of Independent women has taken a turn for the moral worst when it comes to committed relationships.

Back in the '20s and 30s, our grandparents were mainly focused on successful households. Especially slaves; I mention slaves as it being the closest in history that I can identify with. Men and women would fight tooth and nail to stay with one another. They had been torn emotionally, physically and socially. Strong relationships were the pride of families and people. When slavery was abolished families were able to reunite and would walk from different states looking for their loved ones that were sold off. When they did find each other those relationships lasted 60+ years. No matter what background Jewish, Native American, African-American, or even Caucasian European.

Back then relationships were the determining factors of futures and existence. Not once, and I mean not once did you ever hear the man or woman say "I am independent. I don't need no man or woman." Not even Queen Vashti in the book of Esther ever say she was independent and didn't need King Ahasuerus. However she did deny him when he called for her which even then can be deemed an example of female empowerment.

It ultimately led to her removal from the kingdom and replaced with Esther. When she no longer held him accountable as king, he just like men today, left her for another woman. If you are saying men were dirty then and are no different now you're probably right but that would be a bad example and times would be as well.

Most men then went to war so the only option they had were captives, themselves and well...men. Yeah, let's go back because that's a whole other "Why Men Cheat". Point is most guys who hear women say they don't need a man will cheat on the women because he is emasculated. If a man hears he is not needed, then how could you conceive the notion that he could remain where he is not needed. Would you keep paying for a car if it's paid off? No! So why encourage the collapse of a relationship with actions that will prevent a solid one? That's how men see it and that is why men of today really see no need in committing to just one woman.

Lord knows it doesn't help when women are just as bad as the men haha. That is a whole other Bible in itself. As I said before this is just my take on the matter. It should only be viewed as such. All men do not cheat. There you go, fellas, I didn't throw all of you under the bus...not intentionally anyways. Please don't go giving guys a bunch of crap because if you do he will go cheat on you and you will have to ask the all too familiar questions for yourself with conversations that sound like, "Self why did I just do that?" And self will say, "Self because you pulled the Eve."

Acknowledgments

I would first like to thank my Lord Jesus Christ who without my life would have no meaning or purpose. God, I am truly thankful. I would also like to thank all the real and creative influences that made this How-To/Fictional/Self-Help/Drama/Romance/Novel come to fruition. Big shout-out to Tyreem, Samantha, DJ Gabie Jeffrey Miller, Don Castro, Jadon, Trenton, and Danielle Woods for supporting me while I was away. I would love to thank my children Zhynasia, Korea, Tamyra, Arriciana, Mason, Kamari, and Destany, for being the very reason I chose to create a book, to add to the conscious understanding that we can do anything.

I pray, that just this one, of many of my endeavours of life encourages you to place your own brick in the Winecoff foundation. I'd like to thank my older brother Michael for allowing me, even in my creative space, to use him as my right-hand man. I thank my grandmother Lillie for always being a shoulder and a relentless love of maturity in my life. You have helped me grow so much as a man. I would also like to thank Fite, Matt, Deuce, Mafia, SK, and Wade all of whom I met while at Butner. I thank Nick from Butler for supplying me with the paper to even be able to put this thought process into existence.

I would finally like to thank second to none Charia Dillard who without constant motivation, love, encouragement. Support, spiritual guidance, friendship, partnership, relentless faith, and timeless devotion this book would not exist. You are the true meaning of love to not only me but everyone that crosses your path. With all of my heart I thank you.